LEAVE THE FIGHTING TO

McGUIGAN

The Official Biography of
BARRY McGUIGAN

JIM SHERIDAN

VIKING

FOR
Fran, Naomi, Kirsten and Tess

VIKING

Penguin Books Ltd, Harmondsworth, Middlesex, England
Viking Penguin Inc., 40 West 23rd Street, New York, New York 10010, U.S.A.
Penguin Books Australia Ltd, Ringwood, Victoria, Australia
Penguin Books Canada Ltd, 2801 John Street, Markham, Ontario, Canada L3R 1B4
Penguin Books (N.Z.) Ltd, 182–190 Wairau Road, Auckland 10, New Zealand

First published 1985

Filmset in Monophoto Plantin with Impact display by
Northumberland Press Ltd,
Gateshead, Tyne and Wear

Printed in Great Britain by
Richard Clay (The Chaucer Press) Ltd,
Bungay, Suffolk

Designed by Norman C. Baptista

British Library Cataloguing in Publication Data Available

CONTENTS

PART THREE

THE PUBLIC LIFE 93

PART FOUR

DIARY OF A WORLD TITLE FIGHT 141

Part One

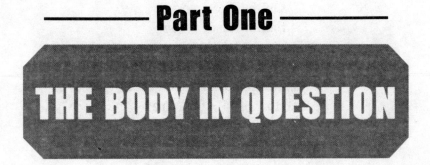

THE BODY IN QUESTION

TERRITORIAL
IMPERATIVE

Our jeep follows a small, powerfully built figure up the steep slopes that lead to the top of Carnmor. It is an uphill climb of about 2,000 feet, over $3\frac{1}{2}$ miles. Somewhere along the way the birds have given up and, once we reach the top, the panting of our jeep in first gear is replaced by a silence that is the mother of reflection. The runner, able to draw breath at last, continues on his journey and without breaking rhythm says, 'You can see most of Ulster from here. The Mountains of Mourne point right, the Sperrin Mountains left. Finn McCool's Stone is about here somewhere.'

People have lived in Ulster for six thousand years. The evidence is all around us: ancient tombs, Celtic crosses, unexplained monuments. Finn McCool's Stone is at the top of Fincairn. People believe he threw it there in a fit of temper ... it weighs four tons. Finn McCool was a giant; he left the impression of his hands on the stone. His tribe was the *Tuatha De Dannann*, a warrior tribe. From the bones of those warriors that have been excavated, it seems that the tallest of them would have been equal in height and strength to the figure now running away from us down Carnmor.

Barry McGuigan is 5 feet 6 inches tall. He weighs 125 pounds, just 9 stone. He has a chest measurement of 41 inches and a reach of 70 inches. His hands are as big as Finn McCool's, and in Ireland he is more popular and better known. He is black Irish with boyish good looks and blue eyes as deep as the ocean. His ancestry is Northern Irish and it has bequeathed him a temper that you would do well not to awaken. He keeps it under total control, walking the world a pleasant diplomatic man – until he steps through the ropes of a boxing ring. Then some ancient strength forgotten by civilized man takes hold of him and he doesn't rest until he gets the other fellow out of there and he goes home to bed. He never throws stones.

Today Barry is on a run. He will cover twelve miles around Carnmor. *Carn* is the Irish for hill and *mór* means big. It is a punishing course, especially if you are carrying pounds overweight and have a head cold. After 80 minutes the course is completed, and Barry rinses about three pints of salt-filled water from his track suit.

'That's called sweat,' he says. He drinks his customary two bottles of Lucozade and breathes deeply. 'I never thought I'd make that first hill.'

Did he ever feel like giving up? 'I never give up,' he says with absolutely no sense of defiance, just a statement of fact. 'I never give up,' he says as he takes the wheel.

Barry McGuigan knows every inch of the border roads. 'That was the smugglers' course we just completed,' he says. Those boys worked by night. The ancient Province of Ulster is split in two by the border that separates Northern Ireland from Southern Ireland. Smuggling is one of the lesser sins that this partition has brought about. 'We're in Northern Ireland now,' says Barry. 'The roads are better.'

His great-grandfather came from Pomeroy near Donaghmore. 'He was the baddest wee whore ever you met,' says Barry. 'Built like a tank. I have a photo of him holding a gun.' It's a duck gun. The gun is six inches taller than he is. He has a long white moustache curled up at the ends. He looks like a bull with the horns coming out of his nose. Every Twelfth of July, when the Protestants would be holding their Orange Parade, he would go out into the main street and scrape a line with a sword. He would score a long line across the main street and stand behind it. Then he would go back into the house to look for his scythe. He would stand behind the line swinging his scythe and say, 'Come one of you past this line.'

Barry McGuigan stands in his home imitating this long-dead ancestor. You can see the scythe and hear the hum it makes. Then he takes off round his son's toys in a one-man Orange Parade. We see the lambeg drum, tin whistles, even the bowler hats. An invisible baton shoots miles up into the air above his home and comes back down through the ceiling, to be caught deftly behind his back. This pantomime ends with the lambeg drum back at the improvised borderline. With a turn of foot that sends many an opponent astray we are back face to face with his great-grandfather. Barry's right hand puts the last touch to his whiskers. The confrontation lasts, spaghetti-western Irish style, for ten seconds, then the lambeg drum turns his back and marches away. 'The funny thing was that all the Protestants loved him. They would be drinking together all year round in the pubs and then when the Twelfth came, out would come the scythe and the lambeg drum. James McShane was his name. He was a wee tank of a man.'

HANDS
ACROSS THE BORDER

Private Leslie Heron watches from his six-by-three-inch window at what for twelve hours each day will be his world for the next four weeks. Home is a three-foot-thick bunker on the Fermanagh–Monaghan border. Boredom is the chief enemy. To stay on the alert he keeps a log of the cattle in McCabe's field. This rocky meadow straddles the border; Private Heron divides the cattle into those under his protection and those outside his jurisdiction. Those that stay constant on his side of the border he calls loyalists and those that stray from the fold into the alien Republic he calls terrorists. At 08.00 hours there were seventeen loyalists and only three republicans, but by 13.00 hours the position was reversed and his outpost shook with the news that nineteen of the twenty cattle were terrorists.

Well, it was either this or the labour exchange in Balham! Only difference is, they don't shoot you for late signing at Balham. Suddenly a sports car roars into view and pulls to an abrupt halt. Three men get out. One of them points out the camouflaged bunker. 'Cheeky bastard,' says Leslie as he reaches for his army-issue binoculars. 'Reconnoitring right under our bloody noses,' he says to himself. He trains the binoculars on the leader of the party. 'Seen that geezer somewhere before,' he muses. He starts to log a description. Small, well-built, dark hair, moustache, early twenties. His two sidekicks start to take notes. 'Regular little Napoleon he is,' Leslie says. Then the three figures get back into the car and head on down the road exactly parallel to the bunker. Leslie notes the make of car: Alfa Romeo. It's now at an angle for him to make out the licence plate. 'That will go into the computer,' he says to himself. The dark figure pulls the car to the side of the road in the manner of a rally driver and is out of the door and pointing at Leslie in seconds. Two months ago the RUC station in Newry was attacked with mortars. Nine policemen died. This could be the same IRA unit.

There is some white lettering on the sleek black body of the car. Leslie focuses his binoculars and reads 'Barry McGuigan British and European Featherweight Champion'. 'Knew I seen him somewhere before,' Leslie says as he claps himself on the back for his powers of observation. He changes the age in his log-book to twenty-four. That keen eye is again focused on young Barry. 'Good-looking geezer for a boxer, got a slight twist in the nose, no cuts that I can see, no scars, not yet.'

McGuigan is on the little footbridge that the army erected in place of the road bridge that they blew up. Leslie watches him carefully put one foot on either side of the border. McGuigan is rubbing his eye. 'There's something in his eye,' says Leslie and he zooms in on them. McGuigan stares back. It's not often you come eyeball to eyeball with a world champion. Amazing concentration. He looks like an altar boy, yet when you really look into his eyes there's something else . . . an attraction – a fatal attraction if you're in the ring with him. 'A cross between an altar boy and the Artful Dodger,' thinks Leslie.

Leslie's binoculars travel down the powerful torso. He picks up Barry's hands and tries to refocus. 'He never has hands that big!' he says to himself. He puts the setting back to where it was and uses young Barry's face to get the focus exactly right. Then he looks at the hands again. 'His hands are the same size as his head!' he exclaims. 'Each one is the size of a great big bloody turnip!' He looks at those hands for a long time. The knuckles are powerful, and from the scabs and abrasions on them they look like he's been hitting a wall for the past fortnight. 'Maybe he spars without gloves,' Leslie muses to himself. 'If he has feet like his hands he'd look like a duck.' Barry jumps into his Alfa Romeo and presses his small, size-seven shoes on the accelerator. 'Ah well,' says Leslie, 'I suppose it's back to the cows for the next four weeks.'

James McGuigan was a railway worker who married Mary McShane, daughter of Peter McShane of the Temper. He followed the railway line to Clones. Everybody remembers his hands. He borrowed them from a man two feet taller and ten stone heavier. He used them to couple trains. He would pick up two thirty-pound chains with a hook and double-couple them. Later he was a signalman.

In the stairs up to the home-built gym there are several blood-stained bandages. At the top of the stairs young Barry is meticulously dressing the hands that his grandfather bequeathed to him. 'I do my own bandaging,' he says. 'I spend £12 a week on bandages. I do two layers.' McGuigan prepares everything well. There are two types of tape which are hung, clothes-line style, on the banister at the top of the stairs. He never rushes his bandages. It's like an actor applying make-up, it gets him into the frame of mind to train. It's a method of concentration that takes him from the real world to that of the ring. He has no time now for anything that might disturb that concentration and he manages to get everybody round him to understand this with the minimum of fuss. As he applies the adhesive between his fingers he acts like a surgeon going into the theatre. And his training is just as clinical.

In public Barry shakes hands continually. On one recent visit to Cookstown he signed autographs for four hours and shook hundreds of hands ... An elderly lady approaches for an autograph for her niece. Barry signs. 'Can't you give us an ould smile?' she says with a face that would curdle milk. Barry looks at her for a few seconds and produces a laugh out of nowhere. A deep laugh of release. It catches the old dear unawares and she finds a smile that takes ten years off her. This she hardens into her photographic special and goes away with her niece's autograph.

After about three hours, three big burly men approach him. They look at Barry for a long time, then the first one puts out his hand ... a proud hand ... a hand that has done a lot of manual labour ... a tough hand that belongs to a heavyweight. He shakes Barry's hand and shakes and shakes, waiting all the time for Barry to cringe in pain. He looks deep into Barry's eyes, waiting for the flinch that tells him that he could break the bones of the European champion if he wanted. It's only Barry's eyes that travel to his friends that make the first man release his grip. He watches as each of his friends shakes hands with Barry. Deep down none of them want to hurt Barry; they just want to show that they are men. By the time it gets to the third man he is actually friendly and shaking Barry's hand warmly. All this is conducted in silence. No need to introduce anybody, just a wink and a nod to say, 'You're not a big-headed wee get.' Barry straightens out his hand and goes back to the autographs.

Somewhere on the edge of the crowd there is a gunshot. It is actually a balloon bursting, but in Ulster that passes for a gunshot. The RUC man puts his hand to his holster and then relaxes. The last of the burly men involuntarily offers Barry his hand again. This time the handshake is different. It is non-combative. It is short. It says, 'We are survivors.'

SHOULDER TO SHOULDER

Barry McGuigan was born on 28 February 1961 at six o'clock in the evening. He was delivered without the aid of a doctor. Any mother will tell you that the pain reaches a crescendo just before the head emerges, but with McGuigan it was the shoulders. He was born with extraordinarily large shoulders.

'I remember it well,' Katie McGuigan tells me with a grin. 'They told me it was a boy and that everything was all right. They told me to try and get some sleep. I felt like a nuisance staying awake so I shut my eyes and tried to go asleep. In the back of my head I heard a child cry. At first I put it down to a dream, but even when I sat up to dispel the dream it was still there like a bad conscience. I asked the nurse and she told me he was asleep, everything was fine. But I could hear it. The little stifled cry of a child crying for help. My child. I knew it was Barry. You know your own child's cry. I brought him home and everything seemed fine. Two weeks later when I was bathing him I noticed something odd about his shoulders. One seemed different to the other. I called Pat over, I wouldn't touch it. Pat says, "I think he has a broken collarbone. It feels like a little step just here."' Katie McGuigan does not attend Barry's fights. 'I saw him get a bang on the head once, and that was enough for me.'

Perhaps the strongest part of Barry McGuigan's body is his upper torso. Maybe it was all the attention his mother gave it after the discovery of the broken collarbone, maybe it was nature doing her magic work, but, whatever the answer, McGuigan has abnormal strength in his upper body. At the top of the old wooden staircase there is a little anteroom that leads to his home-made gym. Barry has stripped down and is shadow boxing. From across the room you can hear the floor vibrate. Now you can feel, you can touch that power which sends opponents sprawling, and if you listen carefully you can hear a strange sound. It comes from McGuigan's shoulders. It's as if somebody forgot to oil them. Bone on bone ... Book this man for assault with a deadly weapon.

The old market square in Clones is one of the biggest in Great Britain and Ireland. Its shape has given it the name of the Diamond. In the early Sixties the Urban Council replaced the old weighbridge with modern toilet conveniences. They also provided outside lighting in the shape of a thirty-foot-high lamp. People would come in to Katie serving in the shop and say nonchalantly, 'Your Barry's up the pole again.'

'I'd go out and there he'd be at the top of this thirty-foot pole surveying the Diamond like a country squire. He was only three at the time. I'd call him down and at that time they had a stay-wire attached to the pole. Well, he'd slide down the stay-wire as if he were a circus performer. He would also pull himself up the pole by his arms and hang on by one arm. I got so nervous of him that I had to ignore him. When people would say, "Barry's up the pole," I would say, "Is that half a dozen of eggs you wanted?"

'Himself and Paul Newell were out the back, and the next thing we heard this unmerciful noise. They had both jumped through the roof of Chapman's the Chemist. Poor old Newell fell right through and landed on the second floor. Luckily he wasn't too badly hurt. When Chapman went to see what had happened he found young Newell on the floor and a big hole in the roof. He didn't know for a minute that there was a second hole in which Barry was stuck. He had managed to prevent himself from falling through by holding on for dear life with his elbows. We knew after that that his collarbone was fully recovered.'

'We finally knew everything was OK the day we took him to the zoo in Dublin,' says Pat. 'We had Sharon, the two boys, Laura and the twins, Rebecca and Rachel. Barry must have been about ten at the time. We were on our way round the zoo when suddenly we noticed he was missing. We looked all over for him and there he was in the cage with the lads with the long necks. What are they called? Giraffes, aye. They're not dangerous lads but it might as well have been the elephants or the tigers. He had gone down over a moat, climbed a fence and there he was at the giraffes' ankles looking up at them.

'He was in his element. We couldn't keep him out of trouble. The only thing that held his attention was the chimpanzees' tea party. The chimps were having a rare old time. The children loved them. One of the chimps really got the kids going. We were seated round the enclosure watching them, like at the paddock at the races. There was a little rail that the children looked over. One of the chimps made it his business to scuttle along the rail and you could see all the little faces moving back like a human wave ... until he got as far as Barry who grabbed him round the neck and held him down on the ground in a headlock. Everybody, children, parents and attendants, watched for a few seconds in stunned horror. The children started cheering and one of the attendants rushed over shouting, "Get that child away from that animal, he'll take the hand off him!" He will if he ever gets out of the headlock, I thought to myself. When the attendant got to Barry he looked up at him with an innocent glee on his face. "Let him go, let him go!" said the attendant, and eventually Barry did. He said the chimp had started it!

'We didn't think it was funny at all. I pushed him on ahead of me towards the exit. He ran ahead and when we turned the next corner there he was in front of one of the cages hanging on the guard rail making faces at the poor animal. I didn't think it was funny and I stood staring at him in silence, but Dermot couldn't keep the laughter in and soon all the kids were laughing. I looked

MATE FOR LIFE

Of the seven roads that make Clones a crossroads, five lead into Northern Ireland. Viewed from any of the many British Army helicopters that patrol the area, the roads are littered with little white crosses painted in some form of durable paint. Time and the elements eventually wash away these man-made markings, and when they threaten to disappear entirely a crew is sent from one of the local councils in that part of the country where the letterboxes are painted red to redefine the boundaries with that part of the country where the letterboxes are painted green. These are the crosses that mark the border.

The corners of the crosses have been joined to provide some sense of order to what would otherwise be rather blunt symbolic crosses. If either of the security forces strays into the other's territory, diplomatic warnings will be dashed off to London or to Dublin. Often members of Her Majesty's security forces will walk past Barry McGuigan's home in Kilrooskey. They will be ten abreast and heavily armed for protection. Fifty yards down the road they will stop at one of the little white boxes and turn back. As they come back they will be able to take in some of the details that may have escaped them on the road to foreign territory. In front of McGuigan's bungalow, nestled against the low-lying Monaghan Hills, the beginning of a lawn is forming. It runs down to a lake that lies as contented as a saucer of milk between the hills.

Clones lies just south of the border, McGuigan's house just north of it, connected by a country road. These are the unapproved border roads. They have seen some gruesome sectarian killings, killings by paramilitaries, by members of the security forces and a lot of plain murder. Whichever way you look at it, the blood is still red and, most times, innocent. Not so long ago, a knock on the door after nightfall was an invitation to a quick end. These soldiers' eyes are peeled. They have been trained to watch for a given set of circumstances. In these conditions all scenery looks alike.

Fifty feet further on, set in a natural clearing, is a small caravan. They have observed a well-built man of about sixty years come out of this caravan every day, get on his bicycle and head towards Clones. What he does there they don't know. Beyond the white crosses it could be a wasteland, for all they care. Every evening he comes home around six. Most days he calls on the McGuigans. He doesn't carry any give-away signs as to what he works at. He seems the outdoor type with a good, healthy, ruddy complexion. He likes his bottle of stout, they know that. The man in question is Johnny McCormack, known simply by his surname.

Tonight he is not at home. It's past nine, he is probably in Clones watching the finals of the Eurovision Song Contest. Barry looks under McCormack's caravan for the rowlocks into which the oars will fit. 'Here they are,' he says, 'now we've just got to get this thing out on the lake.' Ahead of us Bandit, an impulsive German shepherd dog, is making waves before he is calmed by the lake's sudden depth. We can't push the boat to that beckoning watermark and, as if in derision at our dry efforts, Bandit drowns us with an impromptu shower. 'I'll have to go back and get the wellies,' says Barry as he heads back to the bungalow.

When he returns he has a little pup with him. 'I'll put Duran in the boat,' says Barry and he proceeds to drag the stubborn transporter out to its natural element. He gives me an effortless jockey-back out to the boat. We push out on to the lake and soon we clear the reeds that make the area in front of McCormack's caravan a natural harbour. Barry hands me one oar and, as he is fixing the other in its rowlock, the little silver horseshoe-shaped bracket tips

22

overboard. I ask if it can be retrieved, and Barry inserts the oar in the water perpendicular, as if silently showing the water's depth.

I look at our situation with new eyes. The little dog has run to Barry's side of the boat. I assumed this was for protection but now I see that he is trying to maintain some sort of equilibrium as the rainwater in the boat finds its natural level on my side ... I am much heavier than McGuigan. The idea shocks me, not that I have not known it statistically, but I was never aware of it as lump dead weight, which is the way the lake judges us. McGuigan is, if anything, a little taller in height, and I have an idealized picture of myself as being less than nine stone. But I am actually twenty-five per cent heavier than he is. I imagine what that might do to the momentum of the boat and its direction, until Barry starts to teach me how to row.

We are out on the lake, silently and peacefully going nowhere in particular when he tells me he thinks Sandra may be pregnant again. I am contemplating this happy news when suddenly Barry's head turns to some little movement in the reeds. 'Look there,' he says, 'two ducks.' I look and it is three to four seconds before I can locate them against the camouflaging clouds. When I sight them they are flying in formation just like the immovable ducks on a thousand suburban walls. For a time these too give the impression of stillness against the expanse of sky, but then the fingers of a tree break the illusion as they fly in a north-east direction. I wonder towards what apocalyptic vision the leader is pulling his mate when suddenly the order comes to row. 'They left a nest over there,' says McGuigan.

We row three hundred yards across the lake in a straight line, only deviating when Barry has to set the boat back on course as a result of the inexperience of one of the crew. As we approach the reeds, McGuigan wants me to drive straight into them. 'We've got to get right into them,' he says. Just as our hull lunges in I can see the nest four feet into the reeds. I am sure we have crushed the nest as McGuigan puts his hand over his side of the boat.

23

Without taking his eyes off me he produces an egg. 'Feel that,' he says. 'Feel the warmth of that egg.'

The egg is indeed warm and I clutch it with all the protection I can muster. The egg starts to go cold in my hand. It was warmer in the nest. Gingerly, Barry puts it back. We push ourselves out into the accommodating depths again.

I am amazed at how true Barry's sense of direction was. That's eye–hand co-ordination with a vengeance. From fully three hundred yards away he heard a movement, registered its location in the splitting of a second from the birds' ascent, and then turned the boat towards the spot, all the time keeping us on a course locked to his inbuilt radar. By such stratagems our ancestors survived in the jungle. There the co-ordination of hand and eye was looked upon as a divine gift. In that twenty-foot square called a boxing ring, which is the nearest modern man gets to the jungle, eye–hand co-ordination is an asset that can't be trained. It's one of those strengths some men retain from a universal memory, when the eye was tied to the hand not by the point of a spear or a crossbow or the sights of a rifle but by some animal reaction that had been trained to the point of instinct.

'They waited as long as they could before they flew off,' says Barry. 'They always wait until the last minute.'

I ask him what kind of ducks they were.

'Mallard,' he says.

I make the familiar observation about their mating habits.

'For life,' he repeats as we row back to the bungalow and Sandra.

HOLD ON TO YOUR TOAST

Driving around with McGuigan is one of the most hair-raising experiences in the world. His reflexes are so sharp. This innate trust in his body's responses makes him drive the way he boxes: all out, all the time. He flies around the border roads overtaking just after a bend because he sees that nothing is coming from the opposite direction. Added to this is the fact that he can see anything else that moves: rabbits, partridges, hares, hawks and other assorted animals and fowl. This is his territory . . . the fields around Clones. I can't see any of the things he conjures up. By the time I have focused they are gone.

McGuigan takes the world as he sees it. His first introduction to the professional feint occurred when he went away to training camp to box for Ireland. There were four or five other boxers sitting with him at breakfast. One of them made a gesture to somebody behind McGuigan. When McGuigan looked back from the bait, his toast was gone. Blank urban eyes stared back at the country boy from Clones. I suppose it was in similar circumstances that early man trained the new initiate in the hunt in the importance of quick reflexes. It would be no good training a newcomer under the particular strain of the hunt. To be a successful hunter, you need to be relaxed – even with the threat of starvation hanging over your head. To be a good hunter, you have to train all the senses to react instinctively. The next time an important guest arrived in his vicinity at breakfast time, McGuigan held on to his toast before he looked around to verify an arrival. If you replace the toast with money, you get some idea of the nature of professional boxing.

Today we are driving towards Castle Sanderson. It is a huge mansion set in its own grounds. McGuigan has always thought it would make the ideal training camp. On the Wattlebridge Road, just after a series of bends you turn off at the gate lodge and head on through dense woodland. On the road you are in Northern Ireland. Once you pass the gate lodge you are in the South. The woods themselves are a delight, cutting the demesne off from contact with the outside world and yet not so extensive that one ever feels isolated. At the gate to the grounds proper there is a warning to trespassers. The mansion has its own church which sits lonely and abandoned at the end of a field that becomes an ordered lawn within the shadow of the house.

Suddenly Barry stops. He moves his head in that peculiar arc that is the sign language for somebody listening intently. He asks me whether I hear anything. I don't. About five or ten seconds later I hear the sound of something that could pass for a lawnmower. We hide in the bushes. Down the majestic carpet of the Finn River comes a motor boat. Barry wants to stay out of sight because of the notice. He picks up a stout branch and hands it to me, then goes to look for one for himself.

'There might be dogs about. A Dobermann pinscher could kill you. If we see one and he attacks, hit him hard with the stick,' he says.

'What about the tree,' I ask, pointing to an amenable apple tree.

Barry laughs. 'Hit him,' he says.

Later we walk round the Castle grounds, ending up in the fenced-off graveyard that hugs the little church for comfort. In its grounds lie all the captains and majors of the Sandersons and their wives. The little church is still in good repair. What sudden isolation fell upon these people when Lloyd George drew a pencil across a map in 1922! Just a quiver of his hand would have included them in Northern Ireland. What did the preacher say to them on that first Sunday when they left their homes in the Empire

26

and ended up in the Free State? There was as much logic in dividing a cloud in two as drawing the line where they did.

The best view of the interior is from the top of an old vault. As we are looking inside, we hear a noise. McGuigan points up. I do not have the same problem with helicopters as I do with swallows. When it comes into view, it flies in our direction. I note how acute McGuigan's hearing is. 'If you hold that stick up like a gun they will swoop over here,' McGuigan says. I look up. I look at the stick. I think about the black-faced soldiers in the chopper. Maybe their vision is not as sharp as McGuigan's. Maybe their reactions are not so astute. I keep my stick in the divining position.

On the way back home Barry stops the jeep abruptly. 'There's a hawk,' he says, 'on the telegraph pole. Did you see it?' I didn't see the telegraph pole.

All of Barry's reflexes are sharp. I think about the day we went out ferreting. 'What happens is that the ferret chases the rabbits out into the net,' he tells me. All the holes are covered. The ferret goes down. There is a rumble underground. Barry's eyes are flashing in all directions. The rabbits are running into the traps. Close to Barry one of the rabbits comes flying out and jumps straight through a hole in the net. Quick as a flash Barry reaches his hand out and grabs the rabbit in mid-air. He didn't think about it. He just reached out and caught the rabbit. A totally instinctive response.

'There's a rabbit,' says Barry, bringing me back to reality. By this stage I am too tired of this game to pay much attention. I look in the general direction in which he is pointing and I see the rabbit. It's as if he appeared because I wasn't looking for him. My mind didn't say 'rabbit' and then look. I just looked and there he was. Once I stopped my active mind looking for him, there he was. I think Barry's reflexes come from the same kind of attention. Not a logical, rational response but one of a deeply relaxed nature. When Barry said after a particular fight that he must learn to be more patient, I think I know what he means. There's a hell of a difference between looking for an opening and patiently waiting for one. We don't trust our bodies enough. We don't trust our instincts, our senses. We think too much.

FIRST AID

In the autumn, children collect horse-chestnuts to play 'conkers'. The nut is attached to a string, and an opponent is challenged to see who has the strongest nut. It was commonly believed that if you put your chestnut up a chimney and left it there for a year, it would be unbeatable the following season. There were a thousand other ways to add strength to your conker.

In St Tiarnachs National School they played a similar game, only they didn't use string and they didn't use chestnuts. They used their own hands, the arms acting as a lethal human string. The game was called 'hardy knuckles'. Nobody would play McGuigan. They called his hands many names, though none as poetic as the Spanish name given to the weapons of Barry's childhood hero, Roberto Duran. *Manos de piedra* they called Duran's hands in the Spanish-speaking ghettos of Panama City. 'Hands of Stone'. It suits McGuigan.

Dermot is Barry's elder brother by a couple of years. Normally Barry played with boys of Dermot's age at school. Except at hardy knuckles. They knew better than that. One day five of them went out exploring and they found the answer to the problem of Barry's strong hands. In a house in Analore Street they found an old pair of boxing gloves. This meant that the meanest part of Barry's artillery was hidden behind a three-inch wall of what felt like cotton wool. Each of the boys tried and tested the gloves. This was a godsend. They felt happy that now they could deal with Barry. A competition was arranged. Now he had to rely on his punching power rather than his rock-hard hands. With two years' advantage the boys felt secure.

They had made a mistake. Besides strong hands he had enormous strength in his arms. He quickly won his way to the final where he faced Liam Flanagan who shall claim to his dying day that he came out with a draw against the future featherweight champion of the world.

Barry was fixated by the gloves. He couldn't get them out of his mind. During the competition, each of the boys had used only one glove. Because of his age Barry got the right hand. It was to dog him for years. It made him just a little predictable as an amateur because of his reliance on his right hand. From the day he turned professional, he had to concentrate on using his left to such an extent that ironically he almost forgot about the right.

After the competition the boys left the gloves in the abandoned house. It was as if they had stumbled upon some magical adornment that could turn a boy into a man in a matter of minutes. Biologically, boxing gloves turn the clock back a couple of millennia. One of the things that separate man from other animals is the adaptability of the thumb. Because of its flexibility it turned the hand into a clutching rather than a clawing instrument. The boxing glove, developed to combat the brutality of the bare knuckle, turns the human hand back into a paw; now survival depends again on strength. The hand loses its flexibility and becomes a piston at the end of the rod of the arm. The day he tried on the gloves McGuigan knew instinctively he had incredible strength and punching power, as well as hard hands.

If Dermot didn't really believe that his younger brother was stronger than him, when it came to a life-and-death situation he instinctively got out of Barry's way. One day, Mrs Chapman came running in from the chemist's next door. 'He's having a heart attack,' she cried. Barry and Dermot were upstairs, training in the gym. Without waiting to change they rushed down to see what all the commotion was about. Quickly they realized that Mr Chapman, the chemist, was dying in the house next to his shop. They ran out, turned right and quickly up the three concrete steps that accounted for the steep hill of the Diamond. They found the dying Mr Chapman slumped beside his bed on the first floor as if he were saying his prayers. His heart had stopped beating and he was technically dead. There was only one way to revive him. With a blow that had sent many an opponent to the canvas, Barry beat on Mr Chapman's chest. The muscles around his heart got the message. As if in response to a human power-drill, they started their life-sustaining activity again. Slowly Mr Chapman's chest rose and fell. He was breathing again. Maybe he would be a little black and blue that night, but at least he was alive.

DOWN TO EARTH

Imagine Barry McGuigan taking part in a magician's show. He's invited up on stage and sawn in half. The two halves are moved to either side of the stage. Now imagine the magician repeats this trick several times with other volunteers ... and then drops dead. The parts have to be put back together again. Somebody asks if there is a doctor in the house. The doctor comes up on stage and the first thing he sees is the top of Barry's body ... the strong chin ... the long reach ... broad shoulders; all in all a powerful torso.He crosses the stage to find the other half. There are twenty pairs of legs, all wriggling away in their separate boxes. Eventually he puts the other nineteen sets together. All that's left is a pair of boyish legs on the other side. He can't believe that such a powerful trunk is carried by such small legs. He forgets one thing! Barry McGuigan has strong legs and incredible balance.

He has just run five miles round the border roads close to his house. He is trying to lose the extra poundage he gained on holiday. This will have accumulated on the thighs and around the midsection, so Barry has wrapped himself in polythene sheeting at these crucial spots to get rid of any excess pounds. After the run he leaves out his clothes for the wash and jumps into the shower. The difference between the top and bottom halves of his body is extraordinary. For ten years he has worked to keep the weight off his legs and buttocks so that whatever strength he has will be situated in the upper body.

Biologically the big toe doesn't have any of the flexibility of the thumb. Ever since we got down out of the trees it has been used essentially as a balancing tool, an instrument to keep us upright. The strongest architectural structure, inch for inch, in support of our weight is the arch. The human foot is constructed on the basis of two self-supporting arches. One is controlled by the big toe, and the lateral one is controlled by the outside of the foot.

Most boxers rely too much on the arch controlled by the big toe. McGuigan uses both with equal facility. Going forward consists of a thousand little sideways movements that makes it very difficult to pin him down.

Most boxers, when they want to retreat, get up on their toes and back-pedal. Amateur boxers are constantly on their toes pedalling forward. McGuigan never pedals. He stalks. He stalks because he's always ready to throw a punch that way. All of McGuigan's balance and movement is designed to maximize his greatest asset: his strength. He never plods. His forward movement is not flat-footed. All his arches are working. He moves like a vacuum cleaner.

After the shower we go for a walk. 'I tried to bring the shōgun up here last week,' Barry says, 'and she nearly went over on her side.' The shōgun is Barry's jeep, with tyres that were meant to buffer the effect of the worst of terrain. The tyres are thick corrugated monsters. By contrast, Barry's feet at size seven are very small, especially in relation to the rest of his body. To carry such weight on such small pedestals, he must have extraordinary balance.

We come to a small stream, an irrigation ditch that the farmer has protected with barbed wire. On top of the barbed wire I start performing stunts that would make a tightrope walker proud. Unfortunately, most of my movements are involuntary. Eventually I have to jump and luckily I land in quite sound terrain. For a moment or two I could end up in the ditch but eventually, as they say, I find my feet. 'You have good ankles, like me,' says Barry. He crosses the fence with no problem. To maintain the balance he does on such small feet, he must have good ankles.

In the early stages of his career, McGuigan's innate sense

of balance was countered by an incorrect posture. On the walls of McGuigan's gym are pictures of all the boxers he admires: Duran, Ali, Arguello. Some have made it in the British Isles: Jim Watt, Ken Buchanan. The only other pictures are of the Kung Fu expert Bruce Lee and two pictures of gorillas. What they have in common is posture.

Posture is not necessarily something effete. In sport, posture is about finding your centre of gravity. Gravity is the strongest elemental force acting upon us. It constantly pulls us down to earth. Even when we wake up in the morning, we can be up to a half-inch taller than when we went to bed. When the astronauts circled the world in Skylab in 1974, for 84 days, they came back three inches taller than when they set out. Outside of the gravitational pull of the earth, they had grown. To get the body in alignment with this huge natural force is a very important step for all athletes. A gorilla walks with the centre of gravity in roughly the same place that Bruce Lee had his. For thousands of years now, the centre of gravity has been located for most people in or around the abdomen.

What holds the body erect is the pull of muscles in the opposite direction to gravity. When they stretch and contract, they move the bones of the body and complete the simplest of movements like walking. When a baby learns to walk, he builds up a lot of muscle memory that eventually keeps him upright and going forward. When McGuigan is boxing, he crouches like a gorilla, his knees bent, his bottom sticking out. His strong shots, his left hook and his jab, come from below.

Gravity being a field force, once you find your alignment to it, you have a powerful instrument at your bidding. The first feeling it gives you is that of well-being. Once McGuigan had adjusted to his low crouching posture, he felt and looked very good.

ICE BAG

The gypsies have a saying: 'You have to dig deep to bury your father.' Pat McGuigan has given Barry his intimidating stare, his laughing eyes and his mischievous smile. Pat is a musician, shopkeeper, storyteller, *bon vivant*, comic and the father of eight children. It's as if he spat Barry out.

He still plays in the clubs around Ireland. One night recently, just after Barry had won the European title, Pat was setting up with his friend, Eugene McElwain, when he was approached by an old lady. 'You're a good boy,' she said to him. Pat thought she was talking about Eugene, who is fifteen years his junior. After the gig, the old woman came up and said that she'd enjoyed it, then, firmly addressing Eugene, she told him to look after Barry. 'He's a good boy,' she said, 'but you want to keep a good eye on him, that boxing's a tough business.' She thought that Eugene was Pat's father and that Pat was Barry.

It's a long time since Pat was twenty-four but he still has an energy about him that gives him a Peter Pan quality. His eyes dance with the brilliance of eternal optimism. When he tells a joke, you could make a jigsaw from the laugh lines on his face. He's had that many road accidents, if he were a cat he'd be dead. He's been generous with his money, generous with his drink, generous with his humour, but the last thing you should do is cross him. All his collisions are head-on.

The most famous instance of Pat's short fuse occurred when Barry and Dermot were in their early teens. Barry was getting ready for bed when he heard Dermot answering his father back in the kitchen. You don't do that in the

McGuigan household. Pat lost his temper. Dermot saw the flashing eyes ... and away with him up the stairs to Barry. Barry hid him in his room and locked the door. Pat came to the door in a temper – and left it in a fury at his son's refusal to open. Barry was in the cleft stick between obedience and protection ... he chose protection. Pat walked down the stairs; he was gone to get a hatchet. He came back up and hacked his way through the door. By the time he had made it an entrance again, his temper had abated. From an early age McGuigan was a peacemaker.

Dermot tells a story of Barry refereeing a fight between himself and another boy. Barry was the soul of discretion, keeping them apart, even warning Dermot not to be too rough. Suddenly Dermot got hurt. Barry lost his cool. The other boy saw it happening and ran for his life. With McGuigan, you know he is keeping an incredible temper under control. The only time I saw it near the surface was when the question of his nationality was raised. 'If anybody ever called me a turncoat I'd let them ...' He pauses in mid-sentence. 'It wouldn't matter about titles or anything. I'd go for them. I don't care if I lose my title. That would be it.' As a professional sportsman Barry can't afford to lose his temper, or even show signs of it. Temper is like a runaway horse. If you don't harness it, it will do you no good. Without it, however, it's difficult to imagine a successful boxer. Deep down there has to be fire.

McGuigan has always been temperamental about his hands. One night, Barry was preparing for a fight against Richie Foster, one of his great amateur rivals, when a steward told him that the adhesive tape was too near his knuckles. Barry protested that the tape was far from his knuckles – almost at his wrist, in fact – but the official insisted on sticking to the letter of the rules. In a rare display of the McShane temper, Barry tore the dressing from his hands and went out to fight unprotected. He chipped the bone on the third left knuckle, and it was floating around inside his hand for months. It even affected his training for the Moscow Olympics . . . and it could have destroyed his career.

Dermot also has the McGuigan temper. Dermot can get angry. I suppose the games they have chosen show the different qualities in temperament of the two sons. Dermot is a two-handicap golfer. If he so chose, he could be a professional. But his first sports priority is to see that Barry becomes world champion. For his part, Barry dislikes golf. He doesn't dislike the game but he dislikes playing it. I suppose out playing golf, there's maybe three, four minutes of actual action in four hours. Between shots it's all about composure, keeping cool under pressure. You keep cool and then you let everything go in one sharp action. Dermot's temper is ideal for golf. Normally he's a quiet, almost shy, deep thinker, but he's got a desperately short fuse. When it goes he will lose the head, as they say, for a couple of seconds; then he's back to normal. Barry's temper is ideal for boxing. It too is explosive, but hidden under layer upon layer of repressed will-power. When he lets it loose, it's unending.

When Ken Buchanan was brought over to spar with Barry in the very early days, the first thing he said was that Barry would have to get his temper under better control. Most people would never notice Barry's temper. It has been absorbed in most people's eyes by Barry's charisma. It's probably the secret of Barry's appeal that he has such huge reserves of strength under control. People in Ireland are angry, but they get no chance to show it; it's part of the culture not to show emotion. However, it's quite legitimate and perfectly acceptable to let it all out at a boxing match. There you can lose your head. The traditional reason for fighters grabbing the public attention is because they are fighting vicariously for the people to get out of the ghetto. The ghetto McGuigan is leading the crowd out of is an emotional one.

Temper is like a steam-engine. If you give it its head, you dilute the power. It's essential to keep a tight lid on it. It was a blessing in disguise that McGuigan had somebody who wouldn't be intimidated by him in the early stages of his career. McGuigan was immensely strong and aggressive, but Buchanan was the old dog for the long road. He sensed that Barry's temperament could be used against him. He prodded and needled him until he had Barry boiling. 'When you lose your temper, you're mine,' Buchanan told him. He gave Eastwood some advice. 'Whenever McGuigan comes to the corner, warm from frustration, put an ice bag on his head. If he is ever going over the top, shout at him in the ring, "Ice bag, ice bag." And if he doesn't cool down, let him have it when he comes back to the corner.'

Barry has managed to subdue the wild horse of his temper; but he will never bury his father in him altogether. The McGuigan temper is what gets him off his stool to answer the bell.

EVERY MOTHER'S SON

In the late Seventies, Michael Dooley was a policeman in Clones. Often he needed to perform checkpoint duty four or five miles away. If he didn't use the unapproved border roads he would have to drive twenty or thirty extra miles. Checkpoint duty often began at dawn. To avoid any inconvenience, he would dress in his policeman's uniform and then put his civilian clothes on over them in respect to the Northern State, otherwise he might be arrested. Michael has only one other image that competes with his double identity: every morning on his journey he would meet Barry McGuigan out running, followed by the prettiest girl in Clones on a bicycle.

McGuigan might get his explosive temperament from the male side of the family; he gets his discipline and determination from the female side. Katie, his mother, is the anchor of the McGuigan family. Katie is old-fashioned. She still loves her husband. Each of her children is a product of that love, and she will never let them forget that. Barry is the dark-haired 'white-haired boy'. Katie has set all her parameters within the ambit of the family. So that Pat's dream could stay alive, she worked hard behind the counter of her shop. She behaves in the same way with her children. If they have a vision, they must pursue it to the rainbow's end. Katie will stay behind in the shop making sure that the essentials of existence are looked after.

The Red Branch Knights were a group of ancient Irish warriors who served the High King of Ireland. Their training methods were legendary: they included running through the darkest part of the woods without breaking a twig or getting a splinter in one's foot. McGuigan trains towards some such mythological omnipotence with utter determination.

The times of the *Fianna* and the Red Branch Knights were dominated by some extraordinary women. Queen Maeve of Connaught ruled like a matriarch. Pat might give Barry his flashes of temper and his laughing eyes, but when you see the whites of McGuigan's eyes you are looking at his mother.

B. J. Eastwood is Barry's manager. Outside of Barry's family, Eastwood knows more about him than anyone. What he can't fathom is the depth of expression in McGuigan's eyes. He replays a video tape over and over where Barry is returning to the ring after a period of extreme self-doubt. McGuigan's head is down, he is saying, 'I'm coming back and I'm very determined.' He looks towards the camera.

'Look at the eyes,' Eastwood says as he rewinds backwards. Again the tape plays. This time the eyes communicate in silence. There is a certainty in them that is beyond words. Normally, after saying, 'I'm determined to do well,' the speaker would look up as if to seek endorsement in the listener. McGuigan looks through the camera. It's as if the sentence is incomplete without that look. The look is the full stop to the sentence.

Sandra McGuigan slept soundly on her wedding night. At the early dawn she awoke to the faint sound of a constant rhythm. The sound of deep breathing was coming from the verandah of her hotel . . . Barry was doing press-ups. There is no need to say that he has his mother's discipline in relation to training; he also has her determination.

Part Two

A PRIVATE LIFE

POOR PADDY
WORKED ON THE RAILWAY

Clones in the 1850s was the crossroads of the Northern Railway system. In the middle of the nineteenth century when the Empire was at its height the Great Northern Railway (a title apt enough for the Indian sub-continent) connected Clones to Dublin and Belfast and all points between. Oldtimers with the memory of an Empire that extended across the globe boast to this day, 'Sure you could go from Clones to anywhere in the world.'

Pat McGuigan followed his father on to the railways. He was a fireman, which meant he stoked the engine. Smoke signals from the great steam engines informed the residents of Clones that the eight o'clock from Enniskillen was on its way. In a landscape free of industrialization the railways had a mystical power that gave those who worked for them a sense of destiny denied to those who could not travel on the free day-pass to Dublin. The Great Northern Railway also allowed their employees free travel on the other railways of Britain. So to belong to a railway company was to belong to the most powerful corporation outside of State employment. Pat McGuigan remembers with childlike wonder the mechanical genius that was at the heart of the Industrial Revolution and made Britain for a time the greatest power on earth. 'The trains would come into the siding and go on to a turntable. You could push this forty-ton engine round with one hand. I remember my father taking me into the shed and telling me, "Push that train round to there." I looked at him and gave a little nervous smile. "Go on," he said, "push," and I pushed this great big engine round the turntable until it faced the necessary shed.'

With his steady job working on the railways, Pat could afford to think about marriage. He had his eye on young Katie Rooney, the daughter of John 'Papa' Rooney. Katie was a thin wisp of a girl with a figure that would make Twiggy go on a diet. She had long black hair, piercing eyes and a smile that captured the heart of the Sinatra of Clones.

In his spare time, Pat sang with a band. It was the era when big bands were in vogue. The singer may have been the centre of attention, but the band was called after the bandleader, and that's where the money went. He didn't earn much, but whatever Pat earned he put aside for his marriage to Katie. By day Pat worked at the railway depot at the bottom of Fermanagh Street, and at night he would often play in the Creighton, a railway hotel across the street.

In those days Clones was a real weekend town. People would come in from Fermanagh in the North of Ireland to an atmosphere and a licensing law more amenable to those with a thirst. The narrow, steep hill of Fermanagh Street was often impassable with pedestrians spilling out of the ten or more pubs that made the climb from the railway to the Diamond acceptable even to the arthritic and weak of heart. The cinema, halfway up the street on the left, showed the latest Gary Cooper or Cary Grant, and on nights off Pat and Katie snuggled up in the lovers' seat at the back of the cinema on the right. It was a perfectly positioned strategic point because you had total command of all incoming traffic from the entrance in the middle of the cinema and, once in, a patron would get a real crick in the neck trying to figure out who was with whom in lovers' corner. Pat and Katie got married on 27 August 1957. Katie made her own dress, and the reception was a quiet, simple, family affair.

The next time the McGuigan clan gathered for a formal occasion it spelt trouble for them, and disaster for the tiny community of Clones. James McGuigan and his son Pat assembled under their stationmaster, Michael, to watch the last train depart for Belfast and Enniskillen. The Northern authorities were unable to subsidize the loss the railways were making and although the line to Dublin and Dundalk limped along for a time, the era of the Iron Monster was at an end. The next biggest industry, the Clones Canning Factory, closed the same year ... and the boom years were over. Amidst all the other statistics, Pat McGuigan was unemployed, with no prospect of work in a country that was hopelessly underindustrialized and in a countryside that was turning more and more to dairy farming as a means of survival.

Northerners from the time of the potato pickings had looked to Scotland in time of crisis. The journey from Larne to Stranraer seemed less of a rupture than the journey to Dublin. So Pat and Katie, only six months married, travelled to Glasgow.

They still remember Sauchiehall Street and Katie has a vivid memory of the flat they lived in in Ardgowan Street. It was one of those old Glasgow tenements with 76 steps up to the top. 'I remember because we had to clean them every other week. Everybody had a turn cleaning. We lived at the very top of the house in an attic.'

Pat got a job on the Glasgow buses. Not much time was allowed for training and within a week Pat was on his rounds. As he turned the handle at the front of the bus to Castlemilk, he imagined it to be a sleepy middle-class suburb. On Saturday night the bus was crammed with Glasgow's famed carousers. Because of the strict licensing laws, people would stock up for Sunday. The only trouble was that most of them stored it inside their own bodies or in the famous 'carry-outs' that frequently did not survive the journey home. With the zeal of the newly arrived immigrant, Pat went collecting fares. Most experienced busmen considered it an achievement not to be recognized on those late-night-Saturday runs. They loosened their ties, undid their jackets and, like the sheriff in the Westerns, hung up their meters and sat near the doors in case of trouble. Not our Pat. He went collecting fares. There were howls of protest at this late-night incursion into the milk train home. Some refused and threatened physical violence, and so Pat collected those with his sleeves rolled up, left hook, right jab, on the streets of Glasgow. Pat's sense of pride had been hurt and many of the noses alighting that night were blood-spattered.

But then word reached Glasgow that Dave Dixon was looking for a singer for his orchestra. Would Pat consider it? Pat and Katie were never happy in the big city. At heart they preferred Clones and it would be much easier for Katie to have the baby – for she was now pregnant – surrounded by family. About six months after leaving Ireland, Mr and Mrs McGuigan were on their way back. Their first child, Sharon, was born on 22 June 1958.

MOTHER COURAGE

Pat McGuigan was back in the place he loves best, doing the thing he loves most ... and getting paid for it. But it wasn't as sound as it had seemed in the first flush of enthusiasm. It was what you might call less dependable than the railway. The money was enough to keep you from starving, but it didn't come in all the year round.

For the first time, Pat discovered what Lent really meant. He knew it was a time when Catholics denied themselves the things of the flesh before Easter. Traditionally people gave things up for Lent. Pat had to give up his wages. Bands did not play during Lent; it was not done in Ireland at the time. The Church ruled all the rural Irish parishes, and dances were out of the question. If you were caught so much as thinking about dances you were 'read' from the altar. To be read from the altar meant you were a social outcast as dangerous as a leper. Pat McGuigan found himself unemployed during the six weeks of Lent.

Katie McGuigan was now a housewife with two young children and another one on the way. There was no security in the showband business. It was impossible for Katie to go out to work, so with £300 she approached Charlie Slowey who had a shop for rent in the Diamond. 'We opened the shop with very little capital. But I worked out that the kids would never go hungry if we had a grocery shop. No matter how hard things were, the kids always got the best of everything. There was no sick pay or holiday pay in the band business and often the shop saved our lives. We would never have raised eight healthy children without it.'

By the time she was thirty, Katie McGuigan had six

children and a successful business. She got up every morning at half-past six, got the children ready for school and then got the shop open by eight. She didn't close until ten at night. The shop opened seven days a week, and Katie was behind the till most of the time. There is no doubt that she did all of this work for the children's future and there is not a hint of regret from her about her life.

Painted in large letters on the walls of Barry McGuigan's home-made gym there is a proverb which several white-washings have not obliterated: 'Work hard, think fast and you will last.' Barry might almost have written it in praise of his mother. She has an unending supply of energy and a good business sense which she probably inherited from her father. 'Papa' Rooney was a bookie who laid the odds at all the little tracks around the midland. To be a successful bookie you need a quick mind and a cool head. Katie Rooney had these and determination. She has clear green eyes and the type of cheerful personality that suggests a good homemaker. All the Rooneys, it seems, are nest builders.

It was necessary to work hard. The opposition were only twenty yards across the road. They were called the Mealiffs. They were Protestants and although their shop was about the same size as the McGuigans', they had the added advantage that they could rely on their small hotel in time of a cash-flow crisis. The Mealiff hotel is in the middle of the road, halfway between the respective shops. It splits the neck of the Diamond's womb in two, separating two roads, one leading off to Newbliss and the other to Scots-house. Both shops depended on the outlying country areas for their customers. The hinterland was half Protestant and half Catholic; although the Mealiffs were Protestant, that did not mean that customers split in two on a religious basis. People shopped where prices were lowest, and for years the Mealiffs and McGuigans kept up a healthy competition with no animosity.

The most noticeable change in the countryside was the increase in the number of cars. What had been a steady trickle before the end of the railways developed into a flood in the early Sixties. The cars more than anything lessened the power of the local clergy, at least in the area of entertainment. A local curate could no longer show up at a dance and expect to scare his parishioners, because many of them came from twenty or thirty miles away and did not fear a reading from the pulpit. The Church fought its first losing battle with the car in Ireland, and in the early Sixties it was losing at the rate of fifty miles to the gallon. The local girls and boys no longer had to wait on the returned Yank to get an impression of the world outside. Instead it came over the hill in a baby Ford every Saturday night. 'The backs of cars' became the new cry from the pulpits. No Parisian brothel was ever painted as red as the upholstered seats of these new Trojan horses.

The world of the old-style orchestra was in many ways a mirror of the world that was falling apart. It was a world where authority was unquestioned. The band was called after the bandleader and not the lead singer. The leader conducted, and he contracted the other musicians, who played for a set fee. Every musician read from a score from which he did not deviate. The devil's music of the time was jazz, whose improvisatory techniques spoke of a primitive world a thousand miles away from the symphony orchestra from which the humblest dance band felt themselves descended. It was the world of radio.

Slowly this hierarchy began to break down. The dawn of the showband era was at hand. Most of these showbands got their names from America. Pat McGuigan left the Dave Dixon band to form his own little group. They were called simply the Big Four. Times were hard for the six months Pat and his three fellow-musicians rehearsed, but once they were on the road things looked up.

On 28 February 1961, Pat's second son, Finbarr Patrick McGuigan, was born in Beechill Nursery Home, Monaghan. After the initial scare about his broken collarbone, the child prospered well and things seemed to be going great guns for Katie and Pat.

51

The Big Four swept the countryside. Eventually they bought the ultimate status symbol of every showband, their own bus with their name emblazoned across the side. The world was young and the money was good and the *hors d'œuvres* was prawn cocktails. They lived with no thought of tomorrow – but tomorrow always comes. One of the hazards of the road stopped Pat dead in his tracks. He had a bad car accident.

Perhaps Barry McGuigan's earliest memory is of his father lying on two planks in the small room that connected the kitchen to the shop. He lay for three months on that bed, and about the only distraction he had was his youngest son who pottered around while his mother tried to keep house and home together, fifteen hours a day in the shop. At the time of his accident, Pat McGuigan was approximately five feet seven and a half inches tall. He had gone for a medical to join the railway and they had a method of sorting out those under the required five foot seven. If you tried to reach the required height by standing on your toes, a bell went off to warn the officer in charge. When Pat McGuigan had passed that part of the scrutiny a year earlier, the bell stayed dumb. Now, after three months in bed, when he stood up he was only five feet six. Crushed vertebrae accounted for the lost inch and a half. The doctor told him he would never have a normal life again and he would have to wear a brace all his life, like a horse. Katie looked to the shop in such emergencies. Pat looked at his new baby son and vowed that he would recover.

THE LONG WALK

Because of his incredible energy, Katie and Pat had to keep
a constant eye on their toddler. When he was just two years
of age Barry had to go into hospital for the second time in
his life. Katie asked to be shown the cot they were going to
use to contain him; she felt it was only fair to warn the
nurses about his level of energy. A nurse showed Katie the
cot. Katie felt it was too low for her son. The nurse, with a
smile that acknowledged the over-concern of a mother,
showed her the clamp that raised its height and made the
bars of the cot into a virtual fortress. There was also a top
that could be used if the child was really overreacting. It
was like a turf cart, and was usually only brought in for
children a couple of years older than Barry. Katie thought
it would be best if it was used, as she knew that nobody
really appreciated Barry's drive.

Katie herself had incredible energy. She ran the family
and shop virtually single-handed. The pictures of Katie
from this time, the mid-Sixties, are the pictures of a young
girl who was into the latest mini-skirt fashions and full of
vitality. She never looks like a shop-owner or a woman who
has been beaten down by the cares of running a family and
a business.

Pat himself had the same kind of continual go in him. He
also had a strength that sometimes was its own worst enemy.
One night he was coming home from playing at a dance and
he had just passed Naas in a snowstorm when his car, in an
act of self-volition, turned on its wheels and faced back
towards the town as if it was a horse with a mind of its
own. Pat changed down into first and put his foot on the
accelerator, trying to go anywhere rather than be stuck in

the snow. The back wheels spun round and round without going anywhere. Pat got out to see what he could do. Without really thinking, he decided to lift the car out of the snow. He bent down, grabbed the bumper and lifted. It inched forward. Just to make sure, Pat quickly grabbed the bumper again and gave a quick jerk. The next thing he knew, he woke up covered in a blanket of snow, looking up at what looked like an igloo. Cars passed, their headlamps like the eyes of a monster in a nightmare. This went on for some time with Pat shouting at them to stop. The shouting produced a searing pain in his lower back. Nobody stopped. He knew he was on his own.

He crawled towards the car, each movement producing a pain that almost knocked him out and sometimes did. Between consciousness and waking Pat reached the open door. When his hands touched the body of the car he knew he had to get inside fast – there was no feeling left in them. He pulled himself halfway into the car. Then he knew that it was no good: he would have to get the car started or die. He reached over in excruciating agony to grab the foot mats from under the front seat. Then he crawled back down and headed towards the back of the car again. It was this kind of determination and yet cool head that he has passed on to Barry.

He pressed the mats under the back wheels and crawled back to the car. Pulling himself up by the steering wheel, he prayed for a moment before he tried the key in the ignition. It felt like the wheezing of an old man with asthma. Pat stuck his foot full down on the throttle and got a life-saving kick. Behind him the mats were doing the business. The car took off and headed towards Naas. Pat didn't care where it went, so long as it was headed in the direction of civilization. He got to the town and sought out a doctor. He wouldn't look at him because Pat hadn't got the necessary shillings. With the kind of crazy independence that Pat still has, he headed out for home.

Most children pick up traits from their parents. McGuigan certainly picked up his energy from his mother and father, but whatever happened the night McGuigan was conceived the energy was not just the accumulation of his mother's and father's. It was as if their separate energies were multiplied together when positive hit negative that night. Anyway, the boy forming in the womb would have an uncontrollable level of energy. Katie knew that. She already had two children, but some kind of primitive intuition told her that this fellow would have abnormal resources. How do you convey that to a nurse who has seen hundreds of children?

When they visited the hospital that night, the top of Barry's cot was on the ground and he was missing. The nurse said they were looking for him . . . there was nothing to worry about. Try telling that to the seven nurses in the adult wards of Monaghan Hospital asking old men in bed if they have seen a small boy. Eventually he was located at the end of a corridor behind a chair.

After that episode Katie kept a careful eye on Barry. The best thing to do was to try and distract him with toys. On his travels with the band, Pat would see various little toys that looked sturdy until they got into the hands of his son. Once in Scotland he was sold an indestructible little car; it was genuine . . . there was a guarantee with it. During the next few months, Pat had it soldered three or four times until it was finally knocked out of action for good by Barry.

So long as Barry was just climbing the lamp-post in the Diamond, Katie knew where he was. If the people of Clones saw him straying out of the Diamond into Fermanagh Street or on to the Cavan Road, they would bring him back to the shop.

One day in September 1964 his mother took him on an adventure. They went all the way across the Diamond down the forbidden Fermanagh Street towards the crossroads at the Creighton Hotel. Barry almost pulled the hand off his mother as they ventured down the steep hill. This was a whole new world. Past the crossroads, they headed for Church Hill. On their left was the old railway station. They turned right along Rosslea Street, passing over the remains of the old railway lines. Overhead, like a spotted black flag, crows moved in formation as they watched the children return to school. They passed a shed in which the older boys and girls were leaving their bicycles. Past a hopeful litter bin, they entered the yard of the St Louis Convent. The first dawning moment of alarm came when the children were sucked into the building by the insistent noise of a hand-held bell.

Barry had never been introduced to anybody in his life. His mother said, 'This is Sister Camillas, Barry.' McGuigan looked at the figure in front of him. She looked a little like a woman, but she had a scarf covering her hair. Barry wanted to go home and help his mother with the shelves. The only way Katie could get some of the energy out of her three-and-a-half-year-old son was to have him stack the shelves for her. He liked doing that. He wanted to go home *now*.

The Sister brought him down to a bench. It felt like the high chair he had left behind a year and a half ago. It made him feel more vulnerable. His mother was backing off him. Barry started to yell. That worked: his mother came back a little towards him. Barry kicked the bench. His mother hung at the door with the kind of uncertainty that spells doom. For a moment Barry stopped completely. He was used to his father going off – but that happened in the house ... and he always came back to the house and he brought presents. Now his little world was falling apart. His mother was giving him away. She hung on the threshold and he could see the tears in her eyes. He stopped completely as if to blackmail her into staying by his hurt.

Katie went out of the door. She was gone. She wasn't. She stayed at the other side of the door as Barry let loose with a scream that was unearthly. She heard, in the middle of the chest-heaving sighs, Sister Camillas trying to reason with her son. Suddenly McGuigan let out a curse that shocked Katie. She was tempted to open the door and say, 'Where did you hear that?' when she heard another and another and another. Barry had gone wild. He was completely out of control. It hadn't been like this with Sharon or Dermot. They had cried, but not like this. Katie had no alternative but to go.

The nun came to the door. She looked at Katie in a fury. 'Go, go,' she said, and then as they both heard Barry's little feet running up the aisle she uttered what is almost damnation for a nun. 'Get the hell out of here,' she ordered. Katie moved away. She could hear Sister Camillas wrestling with Barry inside. She had lost that battle once or twice herself. Sister Camillas hung on with the desperation of a drowning nun. Barry's hand reached the door handle, only to be pulled back with a final desperate tug. Sister Camillas had a new, strong-willed pupil. Katie McGuigan made her way up the hill. A tear was forming in her eye. She had broken her son's heart; she would never do it again.

THE LONG WALK HOME

It was on an April evening in 1968 that Barry walked the furthest distance he had ever done out the Cavan Road. Behind him the town of Clones was ringed by a series of bonfires to announce the most important occasion in Clones in the past twenty years. A hero was coming home. Slowly a procession made its way over the little Monaghan Hills. People lining the roadside started to cheer, and behind his back the bonfires of Clones glowed in their reflected glory. Like the hero from the film *Ben Hur*, Barry's father waved at the crowd from his metal chariot. The crowd surged forward and Barry lost sight of him. Hands picked him up from behind and without turning to wonder who it was, Barry watched as his father rode in triumph into Clones. Barry wanted to reach out and touch his father to tell him to stop but the car continued on towards the town and Barry followed in the wake of his father's procession. He had his arms around Katie who waved to the crowd from the open car.

At seven years of age Barry started his long walk alone back into Clones. When Pat McGuigan came home from a tour on the road, he always made a fuss of the kids and he would bring presents. Skates were the first craze. The boys would get rid of some of their natural energy on the steep hills of Clones. The town was built especially for boys to skate on. From the Protestant church, at the top of the Diamond, steep hills ran in all directions to the low-lying land all round the town. Across the road from the McGuigans lived the only boy in town who could challenge Barry in competition. One of Sammy Mealiff's specialities was skating. He could tear round the hills and then jump a milk-crate before continuing on his journey. McGuigan was not to be bested. Sammy put down another crate and cleared it with some difficulty. McGuigan put down three crates and went right to the top of the Diamond. He came hurtling down the hill and jumped the crates with a spirit that knew no fear. That night Sammy Mealiff nursed his broken knees in his house across the Diamond.

Barry continued the walk towards Clones, wondering if his father had brought him anything this time. In the distance Barry heard the tannoy playing the song that had caused all the fuss. His father had sung it to his mother in the little kitchen at the back of the shop. He had heard his father rehearse it over and over until he got it right. A part of the song was about a light from above. Barry always thought of an angel when he heard that part. The angel had his mother's face. He always helped his mother in the shop; before he went to school he would pack the shelves, and when he came home he would carry the big sacks of potatoes from the store out the back. He loved the way his mother's eyes opened up when she saw him carrying the big heavy bags. He would race his sister Laura with bales of briquettes. She would carry one and he would carry two, and he always got to the shop first. You couldn't run in the shop, and once Barry and Laura got to the door they would have to slow down. Barry got so good at carrying the briquettes that he never even appeared out of breath when he came through it. 'That wee fellow is my wee husband,' Katie would proudly announce and then when he was gone for more briquettes she would add, 'He's the greatest wee worrier, sure he'd worry about the ducks going barefoot.' He loved helping in the shop.

The crowd that was gathered in the Diamond was bigger than the crowd that had been outside the church the day he made his communion. His mother had made the same grey flannel suits for both him and Dermot. His sister Sharon made her communion that day as well. It was a big day for the McGuigan family, but it was not as big as this. He knew all the people at his communion. In the country all the boys and girls out of the one family made their communion on the same day so that it wouldn't cost so much for the family, but it meant that you had to divide up the money you collected between three.

That day he had more money than ever before. He was annoyed when his mother wanted to change the money in his pockets for notes; the coins felt better but his mother said they would ruin his appearance. He heard people in the streets of Clones say that his father was going to be a rich man after the Song Contest. When he got to the front of the crowd he could see that there were tears in his mother's eyes.

He had seen his daddy cry once. It had shocked him a lot. It was in the graveyard, the day his grandfather died. Papa McGuigan was his daddy's daddy. He remembered the clay going in the grave and the big stones that they had forgotten to remove hitting the coffin. It was at that moment that his father started to cry. His mammy put her arms round him and carried him away. He had often heard that his father was the baby of the family. Maybe that was why he was crying that day. He didn't see any of his uncles crying. They were hard men . . . everybody in the town said so. Maybe they cried on their own, the way he sometimes did. His grandfather had died last summer and he was buried on the longest day of the year. There was a big crowd at the graveyard then too, but not as big as this.

As he got to the front of the stage Barry could hear the tannoy blare out the cause of this sudden enthusiasm. The words were indistinct but Barry had heard them enough times to know what his father was singing as he put his arms round Katie in the Diamond and gave her a kiss.

> One day while I was out walking,
> I saw your face in the midst of a crowd,
> Here I thought was the chance of a lifetime.
> The chance of a lifetime with you.

Barry could remember the day his mother had almost died on the floor. The doctor had come to give her an injection. Her belly was big; the hospital said she might have two babies, and so the doctor came to help her. Something went wrong. The doctor had to ring up on the phone for another injection that would counter the effect of an earlier one. They called this an antidote. He remembers the doctor on the floor saying the rosary over his mother and his Granny Rooney crying in the chair. He thought his mother was dead, but eventually the antidote arrived and the doctor gave his mother another injection. His mother opened her eyes and the doctor started crying. Everything was all right. His mother told him that she had seen a bright white light which kept getting brighter and brighter and pulling her in, until she woke up. Ever since, Barry was afraid of injections and didn't like to let his mother out of his sight for too long. At home somebody was minding the two twins. They were called Rachel and Rebecca.

His father had originally been placed fourth in the Contest, but somebody was disqualified and his father had come third. The competition took place in London. He liked the excitement when the voting came on. A girl from Spain won and Cliff Richard was second for England. Barry wondered what the crowd tonight would have done if his father had won. He would have been the King of Europe. He was already the King of Ireland, at singing. The boys in the school looked at him differently. He was proud of his father, but he was also a little jealous of the fact that the competitions took his mother away for so long. He hadn't seen her for almost two days. He was used to his father going away, but it was different with his mother away. When he felt lonely and alone Barry's mother always put her arms round him. Not last night. He was never so close and yet so far apart from his father and mother in his life.

1 *(right)*. A budding champion: Barry as a juvenile

2 *(below)*. After a victory in St Joseph's Hall, Clones, just a year before he became senior champion

3 *(bottom)*. August 1979, at an international tournament in Constanta, Romania, where Barry was voted best boxer in the tournament

4 *(top).* Helping out in the family shop in Clones *(Star)*
5 *(above).* In the kitchen in Kilrooskey *(Star)*

6 *(right).* Dummy's Lake. Barry's house is in the background on the right *(Duncan Raban)*
7 *(right, inset).* Who is panting most – Barry or Bandit? *(Duncan Raban)*

8 *(top).* Gold medallist at the Commonwealth Games, Edmonton. The hard work is starting to pay off. Tumat Sogolik stands on McGuigan's right

9 *(above).* Work hard, think fast and you will last

10 *(right).* Barry with son Blain, just a couple of hours old *(Daily Mirror)*

11 *(right, inset).* Blain in the ring before his Dad's fight with Juan Laporte, February 1985

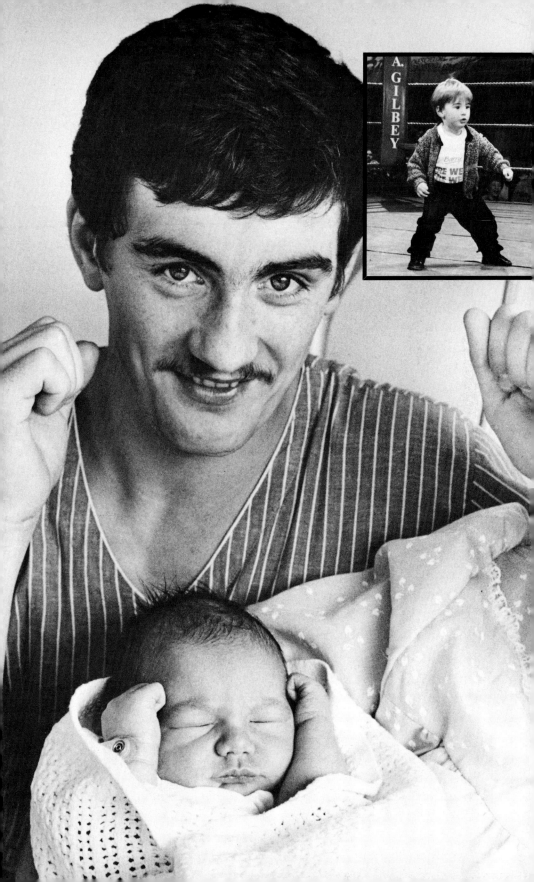

12 *(left)*. Katie and Pat in the gym *(Star)*

13 *(below)*. The record company spelt Pat's name wrong. It was easier to pronounce, so he kept it

14 *(right)*. A training run on the beach at Bangor *(Pacemaker Press International)*

15 *(right, inset)*. The guest house in Bangor where McGuigan stays while preparing for his big fights *(Star)*

The Big FOUR

Featuring
PAT McGEEGAN
Eurovision
Singing

16 *(above)*. Paul Huggins keeping low in the final British title eliminator, November 1982 *(Pacemaker Press International)*

17 *(left)*. McGuigan's eighteenth straight inside-the-distance win, December 1984. It's Clyde Ruan who is looking up *(Pacemaker Press International)*

THE FIGHTING
McGUIGANS

In June 1967 Sister Camillas told Barry that he was going
to the big boys' school. The children were assembled in the
yard of the St Louis Convent and the boys were separated
from the girls. The girls walked in a straight line up to the
second floor of the Convent School. The boys were going
much further. They were going up to the man's world.

They marched down the steep hill from the school
to Rosslea Road where they took a right past the ever-
inquiring crows. Right again at the railway line, they headed
up Chapel Hill. They kept going on past the Catholic
church until they reached the metal gates where the boys'
school of St Tiarnachs had its name engraved in wrought
iron. Inside the front door of the one-level building they
hung up their coats. There were four classrooms with three
chimney stacks. Somewhere in one of the other four rooms
was Barry's elder brother, Dermot. Some time in the
afternoon a bell went and knowledgeable feet answered its
call to the school yard. Barry's teacher led his class out to
the little yard at the back of the school.

The boys' play was different from that of the girls. Today
the big boys were showing the initiates who owned what
territory. Running up to the church wall is a steep incline
that boyhood feet made into a mountain to be conquered.
In the fight for dominance of the hill pupils came crashing
down in an avalanche of bodies. The young boys watched,
astounded. Eventually three boys gained control. One of
them was Dermot McGuigan. To show Barry's class who
was boss they grabbed one of them, carried him gently up
the hill and then unrolled him like a wedding carpet back
to earth. They then stood at the top of the hill, their arms

raised, gladiator-style. Behind their backs on the outside of the church wall young Barry was climbing stealthily to the top. Dermot surveyed the crowd, looking for his little brother. He had been waiting for this moment all week. From behind his back he saw a pair of arms push one of his comrades down the hill. Before he could get there to help, his second companion was rolling towards oblivion. Dermot reached down to grab his attacker by the neck and the fierce eyes that were staring up at him were those of his brother, Barry. Caught in a conflict of intention, Dermot waited until his erstwhile companions regained their composure. He saw their shadows intent on young Barry. In that moment the allegiances of three years changed hands. Political pacts were forgotten as the two brothers redefined the power structure in St Tiarnachs. The school bell called a halt to a new era in school politics. The Fighting McGuigans had arrived.

Back in the classroom Dermot McGuigan made out a family tree. It was the kind they had to learn off by heart to see who should be king of where. At the top of the page on the right-hand side he put down the names of his grandparents, James and Mary McGuigan. On the left-hand side opposite he put down the names of his other granny and grandad, John and Josephine Rooney. Underneath the Rooneys he put down the names of his aunts and uncles (Leo, Paddy, Jimmy, John, Dilly, Sheila, Bridget and Angeline) and his mother, Katie. He drew a circle round his mother's name. Under the McGuigan alliance he put down the names of his uncles and aunts on the other side (Dermot, Seamus, Maureen, Peter, Dennis and Kevin) and his father, Pat. He was called after Uncle Dermot who had died when he was eighteen from meningitis. His father was the youngest of his family. He joined his father and mother together and put down the names of his five brothers and sisters: Sharon, Barry, Laura, and the twins Rachel and Rebecca.

Dermot took a red pencil out of his schoolbag and underlined the names of his four living uncles. His father had told him they would fight anybody. They would fight the devil up from hell and when they had got rid of him they would fight with their own shadows. After Dermot had underlined their names he wrote at the top of the page 'The Fighting McGuigans'. Then he added his own name and that of Barry to the list. A lineage was born.

He remembered his Grandfather McGuigan warning them before a football match not to start any trouble. 'We've seen enough trouble,' his grandfather always used to say. During the match somebody hit his Uncle Kevin an unorthodox blow. You hit one of the McGuigans, you hit them all. From the other side of the pitch his Uncle Dennis came running to sort out the offender. As he went to tackle his man, somebody jumped him from behind and started kicking him on the ground. One minute Dermot remembered his grandfather asking for peace to be restored and the next minute he was pulling a cornerpost up by its roots and heading out on to the pitch to sort everybody out. All hell broke loose. Dermot's grandfather and his sons cleared the pitch of all objectors at the cost of three black eyes and a few cuts and scratches.

Pat McGuigan, who had escaped almost unmolested, was sent home first to breach the fort. Pat pushed Dermot and Barry ahead of him as he winked at his mother in the kitchen. Behind came Dennis and Seamus and Kevin with one black eye. His mother looked at her grown sons and then said to her grandchildren: 'The next person that comes through that door with a black eye can leave this house for good.' With that her husband James came in, his eyes sunk like pearls in the middle of two black oysters.

Kevin had the worst temper and Dennis had the hardest punch. His own father usually got out of situations by joking. One day tempers were getting frayed when his father said, 'Now stop giving out about Kevin. There's nothing wrong with him. He's a well-balanced man, he's got a chip on both shoulders.' With Pat McGuigan the last line of defence was laughter.

Dermot had a lighter which he cherished. On it there was a poem:

> They were made by McGuigan a man named Dan
> In tiny little kiln of the right size and plan
> Their colour when finished was more or less white
> And far was the fame of the Broughdharag Pipe

Dan was his father's father's father. It was too complicated to add his name to the growing tree. Broughdharag was in County Derry. On the lighter was the family crest. It consisted of the Red Hand of Ulster surrounding a lion and a greyhound. The McGuigans were fighters and hunters. He was copying the family crest when he saw the teacher coming towards him. He slipped the prized lighter into his pocket. 'What's that you have there?' he inquired. 'A family tree,' said Dermot as he held up the disposable copy in mock guilt. 'The fighting McGuigans,' the teacher said, repeating the heading. 'I'll give you fighting,' he said as he clipped Dermot on the ear.

Merdie Moore was a schoolboy whom Barry mistook for a teacher. He was tall for his age and he started to shave long before he left the National School. His family were in the coal business, and besides his pocket money Merdie earned iron stomach muscles from carting coal-bags around Clones. His great treat for the new boys was to expose his stomach to blows from all-comers. Having seen young Barry on the hill he was reluctant to take him on, but he was shamed into a display of bravery by boys who knew better. He walked towards young Barry with his exposed belly-button as rigid as a tightly packed sack of wheat. The school gathered round. Barry's eye was in line with Merdie's navel. As Barry looked up at him, Merdie gave a tight smile. Barry was mystified as to why somebody should want to let him hit them undefended. 'You're to hit him there,' Dermot said, pointing below his rib-cage, 'He likes it, don't you, Merdie?' he asked. Merdie nodded assent. Barry drew back and hit Merdie a strong right hand to the solar plexus. Merdie collapsed as if punctured. Barry stood back, ready to defend himself from an onslaught. Over the whole yard silence reigned. The bell for class called the boys back to their desks. To the inquiring teacher Barry heard one of the big boys say that Merdie had stomach cramps.

THE TUNNEL OF LOVE

One day Sandra Mealiff and her brothers Sammy and David were playing in their front room. They lifted the carpet and found a huge slab. With great effort it could be moved. Underneath they found a man-made tunnel that had not been in use for almost fifty years. Slowly they ventured down into the darkness, only to re-emerge wondering where it led to and why it was begun. To answer either question it is important to know a little about how the Mealiffs came to Clones in the first place.

Clones should be a sleepy little town on the Monaghan–Fermanagh border with little or no history. Given its population of just over 2,000, there should be a murder every fifty years, three guards and a sergeant, one parish church with a parish priest and two curates, snow every third year, eight births, seven deaths and three marriages. It is not like that at all.

The Irish for Clones is *Cluain Eois* which means the 'meadow of the height'. Monaghan's nickname is 'the basket of eggs'. If you want to get a picture of Monaghan country, imagine a basket of eggs. Each egg is a little hill. Take a few of the eggs and smash them. Pour the white and the yolk over the other eggs. Where the white settles is bog water, and the yolk represents deep, clear lakes.

Clones occupied a strategic position where you could see travellers from a distance, a high meadow surrounded by water. Although it is fifty miles from the sea, east or west, it was reachable from the Atlantic through Lough Erne. This watery fact would have been unimportant to the monastic settlement that had resided at Clones from about

69

the fifth century, until the Vikings came out of the waters of the Erne carrying their longboats on their backs. The next time they came to rape, pillage and plunder, they found that the monks had unfairly ensconced themselves in a round tower, eighty feet above the ground (the tower survives to this day). So the Northmen contented themselves with the seaports, and the people of Clones remained a breed apart.

Then the Normans had a go about four hundred years later and they got round to building their own monument fort on a site even more ancient than the Round Tower. They chose the ancient fort about a hundred yards away, but they didn't last more than a couple of years; the majority of them retired to the far south of Ireland where, if the climate did not support the vine, at least it was more congenial than the cold of the North. So, apart from the occasional cattle raid, Clones went to sleep for another four hundred years. Then something happened over which it had no control.

The Protestant Reformation was born. King Henry VIII went through six wives and a few beheadings in an effort to adapt the new religion to English ways. The Catholic Church was not impressed by his method of trying to sire a son and so church land came up for grabs. Henry offered the church demesne at Clones to Sir Henry Duke. Sir Henry had problems like Henry's with the male line and the land passed to a daughter, Anne. She married Sir Frances Rushe; but again a daughter, Eleanor, inherited the estate. She married Sir Robert Loftus, and in 1641 their daughter, Anne, inherited the estate. Anne married a commoner, Richard Lennard Barrett, and between them they had a son, Dacre Lennard Barrett. He inherited the land and his family held on to it until the twentieth century. The Lennard Barretts brought in their own people, and so a family called Mealiff came from Aberdeen, and to this day they run a hotel in the Diamond in Clones. It is called the Lennard Arms after the original Lennard Barretts. And that's how Sandra Mealiff came to be born in Clones on 30 September 1960.

On Barry's mother's side, the Rooneys can trace their origins back nine generations to 1500. That's over a century before the Mealiffs arrived in Clones. Not that they would have begrudged the Mealiffs their good fortune. Still, one could not forget that the planters were newcomers, and when the Counter-Reformation reached Ireland in full spate it was only natural that the Rooneys would sympathize with the Catholic side.

For a time Clones became the centre of a European war. There were dark sectarian sides to the conflict. In 1641, fifteen Protestant men, women and children were taken from the church and slaughtered, but King William's victory at the Battle of the Boyne in 1690 settled the issue in favour of the planters. It is that victory that is celebrated every Twelfth of July. Normality returned to Clones but the lesson had been well learned and, some time in the next century or so, Protestant men began excavating the earth in Clones and they weren't looking for gold. Along with the rest of Ulster, Clones became a Protestant stronghold. The majority Catholic population had to live with that or get out. The Rooneys stayed. In 1936 Katie Rooney was born. She married Pat McGuigan in 1957 and four years later Barry McGuigan was born.

One day Barry and his brother Dermot were playing out behind their mother's shop when they noticed the ground moving. Slowly, like Lazarus emerging from the tomb, it lifted. Out climbed Sammy, David and Sandra Mealiff. Within minutes Barry and Dermot were down in these latter-day catacombs on a journey of discovery. What they found resembled a rabbit warren under the Diamond. Tunnels ran from the bank to the church and from the church to the post office. There were even tunnels that led nowhere. But what ended as child's play in Clones had been started by a fuel that has ignited Ulster sectarianism for centuries: fear.

Cut out all the blarney and look at any Irish town, and you will realize one thing immediately: all the skyscrapers are churches. Clones is no exception. The Church of Ireland, as if to signify the corporate power of the Protestants, stands like a sentry at the top of the Diamond. It is an imposing granite structure with a spire that can be seen for miles in any direction. The church was built with the supremacy of the Word in mind, and the Word was 'no surrender'. The Catholic church is equally imposing. It was built in the 1880s by the McMahons. It has a huge lawn which runs a full two hundred yards steeply up to the church door. The image is of a peasantry agitating, by sheer force of numbers, for Catholic emancipation, for repeal and for the land. These separate interests clashed throughout the nineteenth and early twentieth centuries.

Perhaps during all of this troubled history the tunnels served as a security to the threatened Protestant interest. It is said that guilty men were led from the courthouse by way of the tunnels to meet their fate. Whatever the truth, by the 1960s the tunnels' only function seemed to be as the basis for a good story. The reason that they fell out of operation is one of the paradoxes of Irish history. In 1922 the border was established. The Protestant establishment of Ulster, wishing to hold on to a permanent majority, ditched the Protestants of three counties – Monaghan, Cavan and Donegal – where the Catholic population predominated. Clones, with its Protestant hinterland in Fermanagh, became an Irish Berlin long before the Russians even contemplated the wall. As so often then in Ireland, the border was invisible and ran like a crazy pavement all around Clones. It was not meant to last. The British had set up a Border Commission whereby those towns, like Clones, whose natural commerce was with Fermanagh would get new boundaries once the politicians sat down and worked it all out. Sectarianism put an end to all that. Boundaries were created in men's hearts and it was difficult to rearrange them in reality. The border stayed. Clones for the first time in its existence was thrown into what is called

Southern Ireland and this northern town tried to adapt. At first, things went badly. The Protestant B Specials attacked Clones and the Catholic I R A retaliated. Sectarian bigotry reached its high point in the early Twenties. Then the economic reality set in. Men appeared in uniforms. They were Customs men. The invisible border became a living reality, a mundane day-to-day affair.

What happened to the Protestants after they were more or less abandoned by their northern cousins and by England? Basically nothing. Some left, of course. The rate of Catholic emigration from Clones after the Twenties was about eight per cent and the Protestant rate double that, but still in no way could it be described as a mass exodus. Slowly they realized that they had to live with each other. Blood is thicker than water, prejudice runs deep, take any cliché you like and there is one man who can topple them on their heads. He's called survival. Given the nature of the border, cross-border traffic became the means of exchange. Smuggling, poteen-making, pigs crossing over the border, all required one precondition – a close-knit community. So the divisions of the late Sixties and early Seventies never disturbed Clones too much because a spirit of co-operation on the level of survival already existed and it was difficult to shake this. By 1966 the leader of the Urban Council, a Protestant called Bob Molloy, could say, 'The tolerance meted out to me in my native town provides a striking example to other places where the people are not so tolerant.'

So it was natural, when the Mealiffs emerged from the tunnel, that the McGuigan boys did not pour scalding water on them or run into their own Round Tower. Barry McGuigan in fact had a secret, something he had found that he wanted to give to Sandra. 'I found this ring, it was a wedding ring. I invited Sandra down to the back of this meadow. There were these green leaves. Thick leaves, they were nearly as tall as us. We were lying down kissing, cuddling, making love, all the time hoping our mothers would not come down and find us. I asked Sandra to marry

THE THUMB OF
KNOWLEDGE

Finn McCumhaill was one of the *Fianna*. When Kate
McGuigan went to christen Barry, the priest told her there
was no saint called Barry. She would have to call him
Finbarr. *Finn* in Irish means fair. At school Barry learned
of Finn McCumhaill's exploits. Finn had the gift of seeing
into the future. He could conjure it up simply by sucking
his thumb. The first person to eat the salmon of knowledge
got this gift. One day Finn picked up a salmon that somebody was cooking, only to let the hot fish drop back into
the fire. Sucking his thumb to ease the pain he partook of
the flesh of the salmon of knowledge and he could see into
the future. When Barry McGuigan sucks his thumb, he
also has visions. However, his mind travels in the opposite
direction to Finn. All his memories are of the past and they
are painful.

In his last year in National School, Barry was slapped
for some minor misdemeanour. He was hit on the thumb
with a pointer and an old wound was opened. Barry has
been in hospital four times with his thumb. Each time he
had to have it drained of septic fluid and each time it looked
as if the problem was solved ... until it swelled back up.
Memories of the thumb irrigation were so painful that
Barry preferred to hide his swollen thumb. The most
successful way was with his boxing gloves. His father
bought him these after the first time he saw him fight.

There was an open-air fête in Cootehill, which is about
twelve miles from Clones. A ring was set up at the fair and
a local priest matched boys of the same age against one
another. Barry and Dermot volunteered. The boys they
were facing were taller than either of them, as both the

McGuigans were small for their age. Barry's contest did not last long as his opponent cowered in a corner to get away from an avalanche of blows that came from every conceivable angle. Dermot had more trouble with his opponent who was a good deal bigger than he was and who had done a little boxing. To even things up, the priest gave the verdict to the other boy. Barry insisted on getting into the ring to avenge his brother. The priest smiled at the spunk of Dermot's little brother but advised his father to take him home before he got hurt. Pat was stung by this slight to Barry, so he decided to allow him into the ring for one round to see how he got on. Barry came out of the corner like a bull. The taller boy withstood him for a good two minutes until he finally succumbed to the never-ceasing volcanic eruption that rained all over his bent body. The priest separated them; there was no need to declare a winner. In the crowd was Barry's first critic. After the fight he approached Pat. 'I wouldn't let that poor boy become a fighter,' said the boxing expert,' he has no style. Once it becomes serious he will get himself hurt. You should let him be a swimmer.'

After the Cootehill Fair, Barry pestered his father to buy him a pair of gloves. Eventually Pat ordered them from Johnny McCarthy, a local trader. From the day he got the gloves Barry's hands were never out of them; it didn't look unusual to have them on all the time to protect his injury. Eventually his thumb was almost the size of its counterpart on the boxing glove. At night he kept Dermot awake, constantly turning over in his sleep. Somebody had warned him that he might lose his thumb if he didn't look after it. Reluctantly he followed his mother to Monaghan Hospital to have it looked at.

The hospital decided that it had gone too far. They would have to keep him in for observation. Katie knew Barry's moods better than anybody and she was not at all happy as she left the hospital to look after her other five children.

Barry sat on his hospital bed trying to imagine how he would pass the time. The more he thought about it the more he realized how impossible it would be to stay sane without being able to move around. He was wary of injections ever since he had seen his mother lying on the floor in the kitchen. He began to think that his boxing career might be over because of an amputated thumb.

He decided to escape. He asked the nurse in charge if he could go to the toilet before he changed into his pyjamas. She said yes. From the crack of the toilet door he watched her call the head nurse. She pointed towards the toilet. He closed the door. They were talking about him. The game was up. It was now or never. He opened the toilet door and headed straight down the corridor without looking to left or right. The head nurse made a despairing lunge at him and managed to grab hold of his pullover, but she was dragged along the corridor for twenty feet before she dropped to her hands and knees, the drops from her broken thermometer like little silver angels' tears all over the corridor floor.

Ahead, Barry was racing downstairs. The young nurse caught in the middle of flight was urged on the pursuers' path by a defiant head nurse. At the top of the stairs she called to a porter, 'Stop that boy.' The man lost his grip – and almost lost his arm in the revolving door of Monaghan Hospital.

Barry headed out along the Northern Road towards Armagh. Two male nurses started up a Morris Minor as the head nurse shouted at a gardener from the steps of the hospital. Barry knew from the curses she called out that he was in for a hiding if he was stopped there and then. The gardener dropped his rake in his orderly leaves before he moved this way and that to cut off Barry's path. McGuigan had no choice. With the one good hand left him the eleven-year-old made a fist. Whether it was the sheer power of the punch or a combination of their separate momentums nobody knows, but the result was that the gardener was left sprawled on his back with a cushion of leaves for his sore head.

The pursuit continued. It was Barry's hand that was sore

... there was nothing wrong with his legs. He continued for almost a mile until the car came too close for comfort. Then he cleared a hedge and headed into the open countryside. The pursuers had to abandon their transport and follow on foot. Barry kept going until he collapsed in a heap from utter exhaustion. The men who pursued him stood bent around him, each one asking nothing more than that he stay still until they took him back. Nothing would happen to him. That night, on an unofficial visit, Pat promised Barry that he could join a boxing club when he got out if he behaved himself.

OUT COLD

Pat McGuigan bought a Raleigh Chopper, ostensibly for Katie. It was commandeered by Dermot and Barry. It would prove increasingly difficult anyway for Katie to ride in the latter part of 1971 as she was pregnant with her youngest daughter, Catherine. Barry put the bike to good use on the slopes of the Diamond, skating up planks over milk crates in an improvised daredevil course. Soon it would carry him further afield – to his first boxing club in Laurel Hill, near Wattlebridge.

On the journey out, the ride would take McGuigan about twenty minutes as he flashed along the border roads. The road to Wattlebridge has as many digressions as *Hamlet*, jumping in and out of Northern Ireland, unable to make up its mind where it belongs. Late at night, McGuigan would travel the six miles to Wattlebridge, most nights in fading light, then go to a house close to the gym to get the key to open the old abandoned schoolhouse to train. It was a simple grey limestone building whose only excuse for being locked was that it housed the personal effects of one of Ireland's champion senior boxers, Paul Connolly.

Its windows were too high up for an eleven-year-old boy to know what was going on in the world outside. McGuigan trained on in youthful ignorance for almost a year, returning to his parents in darkness. One night he passed a couple of black plastic bags of the kind that normally contain refuse. Inside were the pitchforked bodies of two men. (Time would lay the deed at the feet of drunken soldiers.) Katie McGuigan could not get it out of her mind that her eleven-year-old son had passed this horror on his way home. Crossing the border was out of the question, even for an innocent boy. McGuigan averted the potential row with his mother by falling off a wall on his way home from school one day. He got eleven stitches in a head-wound. For well over a year boxing was out of the question.

With boxing out of the way, Barry could pursue his other love, soccer. He was a speedy outside-right, fearless in the tackle. By now Dermot had moved on to the technical school, but he and Barry often played together in the same teams. Once, in a Gaelic match, Dermot was attacked by a big full-back. Dermot could always stand his ground, safe in the knowledge 'that the old equalizer was coming up behind'. McGuigan had such prowess as a defender of his brother that opponents usually got the message quickly. At all events, the head-wound didn't worsen.

Barry's boxing inactivity was in many ways a godsend to Katie. Now she had someone to help her in the shop. The year of 1970 had been a traumatic one for her and Pat in their separate careers. The Eurovision Song Contest had brought Pat to the zenith of his career. He had worldwide exposure, and a viewing audience of 500 million. He came third, just behind Cliff Richard. Cliff was a millionaire. At the time Pat McGuigan was earning £20 a week. After the Eurovision his manager increased his wages to £22. The only way out of the contract was out of show business, and three years after his triumph Pat quit the business altogether. 'I was devastated physically and emotionally,' says Pat. 'I was playing six or seven times a week for my wages. These were the boom years of the late Sixties when you could take in thousands at the door. My share was three or four pounds out of that. I loved performing and still do, but my heart wasn't in it.' Pat McGuigan did not leave the road empty-handed. He had a lot of bills and the start of a drink problem.

Pat left the band for the quieter life of a shopkeeper in Clones. Quiet, that is, until the results of the bank strike of 1970 became evident. The McGuigans had cashed cheques left, right and centre, and a lot of them bounced very high. The shortfall was measured in several thousands of pounds.

They had trouble meeting their creditors. In desperation Pat put the shop up for sale. John 'Papa' Rooney, Katie's father, had seen more of the world and he insisted they hold on to the shop and struggle through, no matter what the cost. Over the next few years the cost was a lot of hard work.

John Rooney had at least one other instinct that was sound. He would tell Katie, 'That little boy has got something.' When he saw the McGuigan strength combined with the Rooney discipline and determination, he told Katie, 'Nobody will beat our Barry.'

In the summer of 1973, Barry wanted to take up boxing again. With the innocence of a child, he said that he could work in the shop and train in his spare time. However, his mother and father insisted that he continue his education until he got to the Inter Cert. at least. He would go to Master Duffy in St Patrick's High School, who would look after him.

There is a legendary story of Barry in his first year in the technical school. The new teacher, unused to his ways, saw young master McGuigan playing with something under the desk; his muscles were compressing and relaxing in a definite rhythm. Fearing the worst, he went to see what was up. Under his desk McGuigan was using an instrument to develop hand-muscles.

McGuigan was frustrated by the fact that there was no boxing club in Clones. Eventually, in his first year at the technical school, they found a club in Smithboro. It had only opened a couple of months beforehand. It was the same distance from Clones as Wattlebridge, but this time the road stayed defiantly within the Republic.

Time around Clones is measured first in years and then in seasons. Once these times have been pinpointed for their accuracy, the next best time anchors are birthdays and anniversaries. Deaths are measured by their distance from birthdays. The past is seen as productive and happy, not as a time of bereavement or decay. Frank Mulligan, on the other hand, remembers the time, place and hour that he first met Barry McGuigan. 'It was on 13 January 1974 he walked through the door of the Smithboro club at eight o'clock in the evening. I knew straight away he had something special.'

Frank Mulligan thirsts after some Holy Grail of the soul. He has an addictive personality. He became addicted to McGuigan. 'I couldn't say no to him. You can't say no to McGuigan. If you call that love, well, so be it.'

Mulligan and McGuigan had one thing in common: both were fanatical about fitness. Mulligan had seen the Star in the East, and he followed, no matter where it led him. Initially it just meant helping McGuigan out in the gym in Smithboro; but soon Mulligan was up at the crack of dawn and out running with McGuigan. He became McGuigan's shadow, helping to stock the shelves in the shop. At night he often slept in McGuigan's house . . . though 'slept' would be the wrong word. He was like a watchdog, one eye forever on the dawn, waiting for the first stirrings abroad that were his passport to the fields and their early morning run.

Mulligan even got in the same ring as McGuigan. He remembers being knocked out four times in the one spar. At the end of an evening's session he would have to put out the lights to stop McGuigan continuing.

One night the lights went out, but nobody had a hand on the switch. Mulligan was in the ring, weaving and ducking away from McGuigan. He was overelaborating some errors that he saw in McGuigan's make-up. To put the picture into perspective, McGuigan hit him with an unmerciful right to the jaw. Mulligan went straight down to the floor and didn't stir.

McGuigan, alone after the other boys had gone home, started to revive Mulligan. He lifted his head off the floor to try and waken him. There was no movement from Mulligan. McGuigan slapped his face playfully, certain that Mulligan was lying doggo. Slowly, he became worried. He moved backwards to the door and looked outside. There were only two lights on: one was in the local pub and the other was Father Marren's light. McGuigan mistrusted the pub. The road to Father Marren's seemed too drastic a measure to take. Besides, it was a long way away. He went back inside . . .

Mulligan lay alone and unmoved, exactly where he had left him. He went down to help him again. This time he shook him hard – to no effect. He didn't want to leave him, and at the same time he was terrified of just staying in the gym in case Mulligan might be on his way out. He rushed to the door again and stood outside, lost for action. He saw Father Marren's light again and started to pray . . . deep prayers of beseeching. Inside he heard something move. He rushed in and Mulligan was coming round, oblivious to the young boy's growing anxiety.

From the start, people followed McGuigan to his fights, even as a juvenile. He had something that is hard to define. He didn't run through his juvenile career like a child prodigy intent on glory; but nevertheless there was some attraction that made the McGuigan caravan a force to be reckoned with from his first fight; it was an indefinable charisma that was evident to his first real fan. Cathal Slowey has fought a winning battle all his life with Down's Syndrome. He is a contemporary of Pat's, the son of Charles Slowey who owned the shop in the Diamond before the McGuigans. He became McGuigan's unofficial coach, ducking and weaving and showing the people of Clones the latest punch he and young McGuigan had added to their repertory . . . He was the first disciple. In the company of Pat and Mulligan, he would take the promising young juvenile around the boxing tournaments of Ireland. When they got there, the inevitable question was: 'Smithboro? Where's Smithboro?' They were about to find out.

One day the people of Fermanagh Street in Clones noticed something unusual going on outside the local cinema. Inside, men were roping off a section of the floor. McGuigan was making a home-town debut, and what more appropriate place for the future hero of Clones than the local cinema? His supporting player was Ronan McManus from Enniskillen. McGuigan sent the home crowd out happy with a comprehensive points victory. He had one asset that was rarely seen in the juveniles, an awesome punch. If he got through to an opponent, he could knock him out, and usually he did get through. One opponent, however, dogged his early career. Conor McMahon from Ballyshannon was a tough little boxer. He got a points decision over McGuigan. For months McGuigan waited on a rematch. Again he was beaten. McGuigan dug deep into his reserves of will-power; he would get to McManus, it was only a question of time. He trained and trained, never for a second doubting his superiority. In his third contest he finally got through to the boy from Ballyshannon . . .

If there was a wall in front of McGuigan he would not go round it. Eventually he was matched against Jimmy Coughlan who had been five times Irish juvenile champion. In the third round of their contest McGuigan caught up with him and Coughlan was knocked out. His reign was over.

McGuigan was different from all the other juveniles in one respect: intent. McGuigan's intention was to knock his opponent out of the ring. He had deadly intent.

One day in 1975, after a feed of brandy, Mulligan was confined to Monaghan Hospital. He was given twenty-four hours to live. His blood pressure was virtually nil and his kidneys had more or less stopped working. The priest came to anoint him. The one thing that got Mulligan out of bed and out of the hospital was the thought of training with McGuigan. 'Barry used to cry when he'd see me,' Mulligan says. 'He had that much faith in me he hated to see me drinking.'

McGuigan never liked drink. At home, Pat was having his own problems with the demon. The doctor told him he would have to go into hospital to avoid killing himself young. The amazing thing is that McGuigan and his father never had any confrontations during these years. Whenever a confrontation threatened, Barry would take himself off to his room to contemplate. It was during these long hours alone that he built up his iron will-power. True to the McGuigan spirit, one day Pat realized that he *had* to give up the drink. Instead of going into hospital, with its overtones of illness, he took himself off to the bedroom.

Pat McGuigan is not a man that habit has taken the edge off. He can't stand boring routines. He will work at three or four jobs, spreading his energy over twenty-four hours of the day; but if you confined him to Katie's job in the shop, he would lose his mind. He survived in his bedroom because the opponent he was up against had infinite powers of concentration. That opponent was himself. Twenty-one days after he locked himself up, Pat McGuigan walked out clinically independent of drink. It is not a course to be recommended to the normal person. Pat McGuigan is not a normal person.

A FULL-TIME AMATEUR

At the end of 1976, McGuigan had a disappointment. He thought he had done extra well in geography in the Inter Cert., but found out that it was the one subject that prevented him passing his exam. McGuigan is the type of individual who is not at all suited to the Irish educational system. He has amazing concentration, great discipline, an iron will-power and a unique eye for detail, but he is not able to think in the abstract easily. His is the kind of mind that would adapt itself to any given environment and develop survival tactics, but he is not at home in a rigid environment.

He pleaded with his mother and father to let him leave school. They refused and insisted that he get a sound education. A happy compromise was reached: he would stay on at school; Pat would build him a gym. They had an old mill room at the back of the shop which McGuigan's uncle, Paddy Rooney, converted into a beautiful home-made gym. He insulated the roof and built a ring made out of simple rope covered with the tape boxers use as bandages. He fastened the posts to the wall with old-fashioned stay-wires. Two reinforcing beams carried the heavy bags and speed ball. In a corner they built a plywood platform where McGuigan could concentrate on the overhead ball. They put new windows in so McGuigan had plenty of light in his retreat. It was at this time that Dermot began to work out with him.

McGuigan was the only Irish boxer who had a training schedule equal to that of the Europeans. He was doubly lucky in that he met Danny McEntee at this time. McEntee himself was a good boxer, having fought against the great

Nino Benvenuti as an amateur. He refined some of the basics McGuigan had learned in Smithboro. McEntee was as close as you could get to a professional in the amateur game. At the beginning of 1978, McGuigan was still only sixteen but he had his attention focused on the Ulster senior championships. He finally convinced his parents to let him leave school.

McGuigan looked like a boy, but he fought like a demon, to become the youngest ever winner of the Ulster senior championships. A couple of months later, he added the Irish senior title to that honour, and he was chosen to represent Northern Ireland at the Commonwealth Games in Edmonton, Alberta. The sight of the baby-faced McGuigan fighting Tumat Sogolik from Papua New Guinea in the final was astonishing. Sogolik had knocked out all his opponents up to that fight, but McGuigan went after him as if he was the one going to do the knocking out. McGuigan was forced to take two counts but he continued going after Sogolik, scoring all the time, and got the decision to become the youngest ever Commonwealth champion. It seemed that McGuigan could never be beaten in the amateur game.

One night in the summer of 1979, Sandra got her usual phone-call from Barry after a fight abroad. In the background she could hear the crowd shouting a corrupt version of Barry's name. She couldn't quite make out what Barry was saying – he was very close to tears. He had been beaten for the first time as a senior boxer. The Russian, Gladychev, had got the decision over him. There was another fight in progress in the European Juniors in Rimini, but the crowd were keeping up a violent demonstration against the decision in Barry's contest.

Sandra could not believe it; in her mind Barry was unbeatable. He had won gold medals in multi-nation tournaments in Holland and Romania against opponents with twice his experience. Sandra asked Barry whether he had fought well. Barry replied that he had fought the best fight of his life. The judges had voted two-all and then the French judge cast his vote in favour of the Russian. Gladychev went on to win the gold medal, but that was little consolation to Barry. As a sop, his contest was voted 'fight of the tournament'. All the Irish contingent felt that there had been a miscarriage of justice.

Early in 1980, McGuigan accompanied his father to London. Pat was going to see a Harley Street specialist, and Barry was going to take the opportunity to find out what it would be like sparring with the professionals. To discover why Pat wanted to see the best doctors in the world, you have to go back to a day in September, 1979.

'My mother woke me out of my sleep one night at the end of September 1979. "It's your father," she said. "There's been an accident." I asked her to tell me straight. I knew it was serious by the look on her face. I'll never forget it, it was the day the Pope came to Ireland. Eventually I said, "Is Papa dead?" "No," she said, "he's alive." He was alive barely.'

Pat McGuigan had fallen asleep on the Monaghan Road on the way to Clones. When he woke up, the car, was on the grass verge, a couple of hundred yards from Clones, and heading straight for a tree. 'I woke up for one second just before impact. The car took away a few of the posts before hitting the tree. I went straight through the window and hit the tree with my face. Then the car turned over on its back and the driver and I were unconscious. When I came to, the first thing I did was turn off the engine. I kept thinking we were going to burst into flames. I crawled over the driver and got out of the car through the window. When the police came he was still in the upturned car, held firmly in place by his safety belt. The roof where I had been was completely caved in. Had I been wearing a safety belt, I was dead.'

Pat brought McGuigan to the gym where Charlie Magri was training. Charlie Magri was a brilliant professional boxer, soon to be world champion. McGuigan sparred with him and Magri was not seen in a ring for six months afterwards. He had suffered a broken nose.

The only thing that kept McGuigan in the amateur game was the prospect of the Olympic Games for which he was chosen as Ireland's captain. As an amateur McGuigan overtrained. The Irish boxing officials took him away from his home base and kept him and the other boys in confinement at Drogheda. If McGuigan said he had done fifty rounds training the officials told him to do another fifty. McGuigan took them at their word.

After getting through the first contest against a man from Tanzania, he was beaten by Wilfred Kabunda from Zambia. Kabunda was a tall rangy boxer and McGuigan had not yet perfected the body shots that would reduce such opponents to his size. But he should still have beaten Kabunda, who was not in his league, and in his defeat Ireland lost the best prospect for a gold medal they had ever had in boxing.

Winning gold medals at the modern Olympics is a full-time occupation. It was only with time and professional experience that trainers could find out that their job would be to stop Barry training to keep him fresh. All through the Olympic preparations and the events themselves, McGuigan couldn't get one image out of his mind; that image had dark-brown eyes and black hair. Sandra Mealiff, his childhood sweetheart, had grown into a beautiful woman. McGuigan was mad about her for years but was afraid to ask her out, fearing a rejection. Sandra kept her interest under wraps for as long as she could. When McGuigan asked her out to a disco in the early part of 1979, she was delighted to go with him. Soon she would be at his side, night, noon and morning ... early morning. McGuigan got up at dawn to train and Sandra was always there, counting the number of punches he threw in a round.

While he was in Moscow for the Olympics, McGuigan saved all his expenses for the engagement ring he was going to buy Sandra when he returned home. A couple of weeks after he got back, McGuigan proposed, and Sandra agreed.

Apart from working in the shop, the only other real way Barry could think of to support a family was as a professional boxer. His mother would be against that decision ... but Barry knew if he broke the news to her gently, then she would not go against his wishes.

Part Three

THE PUBLIC LIFE

SOUTH OF THE BORDER

Bernard Joseph 'Barney' Eastwood had seen Barry McGuigan on TV. He was instantly struck by his courage and stamina, but deep down at a different level he recognized some quality in McGuigan that others couldn't see. He knew for certain that McGuigan was as territorial inside the ring as he himself was outside it. Divine instinct told him they would make a great team. He went to see McGuigan fight in the amateurs, and let it be known that he was interested. So was McGuigan. They arranged a meeting in the Ballymascanlon Hotel in Dundalk. Barry would be there with his father, Pat.

Eastwood travelled to the meeting with his old friend Davey Donnelly, 'Davey the Hat' as he was known. Donnelly and Eastwood talked for a time about McGuigan as a prospect. Eastwood was convinced that the young fighter needed more than the three rounds of amateur boxing to be at his best, but the question still remained: was McGuigan good enough to hang the revival of professional boxing in Belfast around his neck? Davey asked Eastwood why he thought so much of the young man from Clones. Eastwood pointed to his chest and then, as he made a circle that encompassed his upper body, said, 'He has a heart that big.' For a time he and Davey fell silent. As they approached the border, Eastwood's mind went back to his first encounter with boxing. It was during the Second World War.

Eastwood was a boy of seven in 1939. It was terrible ... everything was rationed. All you got were rations, and rations was what was left when you took the fun out of life. Sugar was in short supply and people started making imitation sweets that tasted awful. Barney, the little boy, thought it was the same all over. Then his mother told him about Dublin. Dublin was over the border. The people in Dublin were not at war with the Germans. Dublin in the early 1940s was like an unending bazaar to a small boy from Northern Ireland. He stayed with his mother in a hotel called Wynns and the furthest they walked was round the corner to Clearys where you could buy all sorts of stuff that had not been on sale for ages where he lived. Every day he asked his mother the same thing. Every day she refused. At the end of their week's holiday in a fit of extravagance she bought him the boxing gloves he coveted.

On the train home his mother was very nervous, he didn't know why. They were stopped at the border at a place called Gorawood. Men in uniform got on the train. They would ask people to open their bags, and then pass on. When they came to Barney's mother they asked her to get out on the platform. They were joined by more men in uniform. Their bags were emptied. The men started to take away all the things his mother had bought for the house, even some of the things she had brought with her to Dublin. They even took her watch. Barney held on to his parcel. The man in uniform asked him to open it. He refused. The man insisted. He hung on to his present for dear life. Eventually the man pulled it from him but Barney held on to one glove. The man tore the wrapping off the other glove and said that he would have to confiscate them. Barney still wouldn't let go. One of the other men in uniform said, 'Let the boy have the gloves,' and thus was born B. J. Eastwood's love for boxing.

The meeting in the Ballymascanlon Hotel was something of a formality. Each party had decided in advance that they wanted to work with the other. All that remained to be ironed out were the little nagging questions each side wanted to ask about the other. When Pat McGuigan was on the road showband managers suddenly found out that a hit record could get you three to four times your normal appearance fees. It only took a couple of thousand records sales to get you into the charts, and ten thousand would

96

make you number one. So within a few years managers' garages were full of awful records that nobody wanted. To get to the top of the international charts, these little Caesars reckoned all you needed was a garage big enough to hold all the records. So Pat was wary of little men who talked big and asked you to sign on the dotted line.

But the first signs from Eastwood were encouraging. He offered no fat contracts; all he offered were his services. So far so good. Pat and Barry had a vision. They asked Eastwood whether he shared it. Yes, Eastwood answered, Barry could be world champion. All it needed was organization.

If business structures are organized around will-power, then Eastwood's business was on a sound footing. He had started from his mother's little shoe shop in Cookstown, bought his own pub in Carrickfergus at the age of twenty, and by his mid-thirties he owned the biggest string of betting shops in Northern Ireland. By the time he reached the half-century he was becoming tired of his gambling empire and needed something to stretch his iron will-power and business brain.

He asked McGuigan what he would have to drink. Barry would have a soda water and Pat would have a watered soda. They couldn't be prevailed upon to indulge in the traditional Irish toast to the beginning of a partnership. Barry, it turned out, had rarely been in a pub in his life and had never once had an alcoholic drink. Eastwood was delighted: he had seen many a venture come a cropper under the guidance of the demon drink. Barry told Eastwood he would never drink. Eastwood was very impressed: he recognized will-power.

Before he left, Eastwood told Barry that he wanted him to think about what he was doing. He would give him as long as he wanted; he didn't want him to rush into anything. Pat asked Eastwood about strategy. Eastwood replied that no expense would be spared to get Barry to the top. He would have the best coaches and trainers. Money for Barry himself would be scarce at the beginning but, if Barry succeeded, then the rewards would be huge. It all depended on Barry being a winner.

They shook hands and walked out to the car park. Eastwood got into his Rolls-Royce. Everything about this man was impressive. The McGuigans asked themselves what he knew about boxing.

Eastwood had learned his entrepreneurial trade at about eight years of age. During the war, the American troops who were stationed in Norhtern Ireland staged boxing tournaments. They quickly developed a liking for young Eastwood as he knew the lie of the land. He had no scruples about getting the servicemen the odd small bottle of whiskey that they wanted. If any of the locals wanted tickets for the army boxing, the man to see was the boy Eastwood.

The army had a scouting policy whereby they found the best amongst the local youth and had them spar with each other. Eastwood was able to hold his own against his opponents except for one young chap called Murphy. Contests between these two brought the neighbours from far and wide. Eastwood could never understand why he couldn't beat him. One day he was explaining his dilemma to a Texan who smoked Camel cigarettes. 'It's because you both are southpaws,' said the American. Eastwood, still a boy, didn't know what a southpaw was. 'A southpaw is an unorthodox fighter,' explained the soldier. 'He stands with his right foot forward. Murphy is a southpaw, the same as you. He must have the same difficulty beating you as you do beating him.'

Thus was born Eastwood's respect for coaching and tactics. He is always willing to listen. He also knew that boxing had to be organized just like any other business. The army cards were top class, with the odd professional thrown in for good measure. People came from near and far to see the contests. It was an escape from the austerity of the war. Now Belfast was in the middle of another war. It had gone on twice as long as the Second World War and people were tired of it. They needed some outlet, and Eastwood was going to give it to them. He was a gambler.

He was staking all on one young man from Clones, a man with the heart of a lion but still with a long way to go. Eastwood would give him all the help he could.

Eastwood went home that night, convinced of a fairy-tale dream that depended in the first instance on a phone-call from Clones. He didn't have long to wait. The McGuigans had made up their minds before they arrived back in Clones. They would go with Eastwood.

In March 1981 the contract was signed.

ON THE ROAD

Two roads lead out of Clones to the world. One goes to Dublin and the other to Belfast. Pat McGuigan took the road to Dublin. It brought him eventually to the summit of his fame at the Eurovision Song Contest in London. Dublin had a more cosmopolitan atmosphere than Belfast. It had once been the second largest city in the British Isles, the capital of colonial Ireland, and it was from its environs that ambitious people went on to greater fortune. Now Belfast was in the middle of the troubles. For a time in the early Seventies most people equated playing in Belfast with playing in Beirut or Hanoi ... a place to be avoided if at all possible. The people of Belfast, however, hungered for diversion. They needed a hero they could all get behind. In the first year of the Eighties, Belfast was beginning to come out of the doldrums, and Barry McGuigan came along that road from Clones at just the right time.

Barry hadn't been long in the city when Eddie Shaw, his new trainer, asked him home to tea. Barry had been to Belfast to train for the amateurs but he had never spent much time in it. Belfast in the mid-Seventies was not a place you loitered in, with or without intent. Barry followed Eddie to the bus that would take them up the Falls Road. Parallel with the Catholic Falls is the Protestant Shankill. Both of them run steeply towards the mountains that surround Belfast as if panting for breath. These are the mean streets of Belfast. The city itself has one of the best settings imaginable, lying between an expansive lough and the Divis Mountains.

The problem with the city is that it grew up too quickly. In the middle of the last century, people poured into it from the famine-starved countryside at a rate that saw Belfast double its population every decade. Catholic and Protestant workers were housed within the narrowest of confines. They had enough in common to join together in 1906 in a common strike. Today, as Barry journeys to the upper Falls, he will see the invisible border at Clones made manifest in the barricade that separates the embittered communities. Rocks that seem to have rolled down the mountain in a flow of lava stand at the various pubs doing mute sentry duty against car bombers. The street-names on the lower Falls have been converted to Irish, but the murals that are being painted need no decoding. Belfast is in the middle of a hunger strike and you could shave yourself against the tension in the air.

Mary, Eddie's wife, has the tea ready and Barry looks around at the collection of medals and cups that Eddie won as an amateur fighting for Ireland. In one corner is a memento of Eddie's reign as bantamweight champion of Ulster, seventeen years before McGuigan. Tonight McGuigan will stay with Eddie. Tomorrow they go to Dublin. Ever since McGuigan came to Belfast, Eastwood has tried to make the conditions as close as possible to home. Hollywood, County Down, is the kind of place where the houses as well as the people have names. McGuigan has stayed with the Eastwood family at their home on the sweet lough slopes. Frances Eastwood treated McGuigan like one of her own children. The change is not too abrupt from the townland of Clones. Every evening as he leaves Gortnagreen to train in his grandfather's boots, McGuigan can see the odd hillside lamp on the opposite shore sweep down into a riotous assembly of light around Belfast.

Tonight he's part of that illumination as Eddie Shaw takes him in a taxi to the National Forresters Club at the bottom of the Falls Road. There he will meet the beginning of his Belfast fan-club; these men know their boxing. Eddie himself is from the Immaculata Club which produced two Irish medal-winners at the Olympics. As the night goes on, the company will be swelled by men who were themselves boxers: Barney Wilson as a professional was looked after by Eastwood; Jim Jordan was an Ulster senior champion. Eddie introduces Sean Feeney who will drive him to Dublin. On 10 May they are joined by Ned McCormack and Daniel Mulleady, and they set off towards Dublin in a Renault 16 to conquer the world.

At his first fight Barry witnessed the cruel reality of professional boxing. Headlining the bill was Charlie Nash of Derry. His thirtieth birthday fell on 10 May. On that May night in Dalymount Park in the open air his professional career virtually came to an end. A year previously in a world title fight he had Jim Watt of Scotland on the floor, only to be stopped himself in the fourth round. Tonight he was defending his European title against Joey Gililisco of Spain. He took a bad beating before he was knocked out in the sixth round. Nash spent his thirtieth birthday in a Dublin hospital.

It was up to McGuigan to provide some sort of comfort to the open-air spectators. He was fighting Selvin Bell. By the end of the first round he had weighed his opponent up, and he came out in the second determined to finish the fight. Some good left hooks caught Bell in a corner before he was almost bent double with a vicious right to his body. Bell fell through the ropes and McGuigan almost followed him in his eagerness. The referee jumped in to save Bell. The fight was over in the second round.

Barry McGuigan's next fight was on a bill even higher up the ladder of professional boxing. Eastwood had managed to get him on to a world title fight bill. Jim Watt was defending his lightweight title at Wembley Pool against Alexis Arguello. The Eastwood camp wanted McGuigan to take it easy in the first few rounds of his fight with Gary Lucas. By the start of the third they could restrain him no longer, and by the fourth round Lucas was cowering under a barrage of blows. Again the referee stopped the fight.

Now Eastwood had a problem. Watt had been defeated, and there were very few prospective top-class bills to which he could attach McGuigan. Going to America was out of the question for the time being. They had to find a matchmaker closer to home. Eastwood had known Paddy Byrne since the early Sixties. Paddy was an affable Dubliner who had worked his way to a respected career in boxing after starting life as a paper-seller on the streets of Dublin. He made a match in the UK for McGuigan against a good young boxer called Peter Eubanks in the fighter's home-town of Brighton.

Eastwood and McGuigan learned more from the Eubanks fight than they did from twenty subsequent bouts. Lesson number one: never again would McGuigan fight two-minute rounds. McGuigan's biggest asset was his strength. He hadn't enough time in two minutes to get to his opponent and, when he did knock Eubanks down in the second round, there wasn't enough time to finish him off. Lesson number two: fighting in the opponent's home-town can be dangerous. The inspiration the crowd gives to the home-town fighter can just be enough to shade the decision in his favour. Eubanks won the fight by half a point. Lesson number three: to get anywhere in the fight game you have to be one hundred and one per cent fit. In the seventh and eighth rounds McGuigan slowed down. After being ahead early on, it was probably this image of a tiring McGuigan that swung the decision in Eubanks' favour. Lesson number four: Paddy Byrne was a good matchmaker. The next fight would be in Belfast. They had to take the bull by the horns. Jean Marc Renard was a world-class boxer . . . Eight three-minute rounds.

There is no such thing as a right or wrong style in boxing; there is only the most effective style. At this stage in his career McGuigan was ineffective defensively. He stood too upright so that his centre of gravity was often misplaced. He walked forward instead of stalking. Often his legs were parallel. There is nothing wrong with any of this unless you get hit. In his fight with Renard, McGuigan got hit with a good right. He was walking on to the punch and he was totally off balance. He hit the deck. He was up as quick as he went down and had the presence of mind to head straight for a neutral corner. McGuigan recovered from the knockdown to win convincingly. Once he got inside Renard's defence he caught him repeatedly with short sharp punches.

The Eubanks and Renard fights were extremely good for McGuigan psychologically: they lifted pressure off his shoulders. No longer would he have to defend an unbeaten professional record, and he had been to the canvas, and recovered to win. They proved that he had the mental resources to be a champion. After the Eubanks decision, which was considered unjust by many ringside commentators, McGuigan was in tears. Alone in the dressing room, Eastwood tried to console him.

After McGuigan had listened for a time he looked Eastwood in the eye. 'Do you think I can be world champion?' he asked.

'Yes,' said Eastwood, 'and I was never more sure than tonight.'

McGuigan stopped crying. He wouldn't do that again in public for four years.

FAMINE LACE

Sandra Mealiff had a special piece of lace she wanted worked into a dress. The only person who knew how to adapt Clones lace lived on the slopes of Carnmor. Clones lace was a craft forgotten for two or three generations around Clones.

After the famine, an English lady attached to the local Protestant church introduced the idea as a way of making some hard-earned cash from a cottage industry. What was a piece of finery to the rest of the world was a method of survival to the people around Clones. The intricacy of the work demanded daylight. The starving countryfolk worked by any light they could get until their own light faded. To be directed to the person who knew most about the delicate cloth was to be directed to a blind lady. Survival was through the eye of the needle. Eventually the industry collapsed. People were no longer literally starving and the only people making real money out of it were the middlemen. There are many stories as to why it actually collapsed. One version is that a rich aristocratic British lady saw the pain inflicted by the art and made the lace as unwelcome on the mainland as Jewish oranges in Iran. This version is mostly associated with Protestant opinion around Clones. The Catholic version would be that once the people no longer needed the art just to stay alive, it became something associated with the famine and meant that only families that were actually down and out would contemplate letting their daughters near it. Clones lace was stigmatized.

The dress that Sandra Mealiff wanted to work the lace into was her wedding dress. It says something about her attitude to the past: she doesn't live in it . . . neither does Barry. He wasn't interested in attitudes to him marrying a Protestant. He was in love with Sandra and that was that. To Barry and Sandra, too many people used the past to justify the unhappy way they lived in the present. Very few had a vision of the future. Barry and Sandra saw their future together and they weren't going to let anybody stand in their way. They would be married in a Protestant church and the children would be brought up Catholic. End of story.

Only two people stood in Barry's way. One of them was from Puerto Rico. His name was Terry Pizarro. The other was Peter Eubanks. Barry had to avenge that defeat before he could get married in peace.

Eastwood decided that Ken Buchanan could teach McGuigan a lot about the fight game, and so he brought him over to Belfast to eradicate some of McGuigan's faults. From his amateur days McGuigan had a habit of turning his left hook in just before impact, as if it was a screwdriver. Buchanan asked him why; McGuigan had no answer. All it meant was that the impact of the punch was reduced and the area of the fist that actually landed was limited. Buchanan became something of a father-figure to McGuigan, teaching him to keep his temper in check and correcting mistakes in his posture and stance. Every time McGuigan threw a left hook, Buchanan hit him below the heart. McGuigan thought about that.

The Ulster Hall is a cavernous building near the centre of Belfast. With its old-style pipe organ, it's the kind of place you would expect to see a religious revivalist meeting taking place. The revival Eastwood was after was of a secular nature. Everything was done to get the crowds out. At the first contest in the hall a lot of the old-time fight fans had turned out. They liked what they saw. They would be back. Eastwood had filled the hall for the Renard fight, though not all the tickets had been sold! McGuigan's second opponent in Belfast was an unknown quantity. He soon made himself well known. 'Terrible' Terry Pizarro could talk up a storm, and he filled the hall.

Eastwood told Pizarro he would put up his picture all over his office if he knocked McGuigan out as he had boasted. As the old Jack Solomons fanfare played, Pizarro stepped into the ring. McGuigan followed, with Eastwood, the promoter, in dinner jacket. When he was introduced, Pizarro danced out backwards like a Roman gladiator. That was the best part of his performance. When McGuigan hit him a few times in the first round Pizarro put his gloves up to his head to protect himself. The only problem was that if he kept them there he couldn't hit McGuigan. The referee warned him that he would have to put up a fight. His method of doing this was to throw lefts and rights ... together ... like a demented oarsman with the water coming up over his head. McGuigan toyed with him and Pizarro was happy when the referee stopped it in the fourth round. McGuigan's body shots, he said, were 'lethal'. After the Pizarro contest there was only one fight that would fill the Ulster Hall with an expectant Belfast crowd: the return with Peter Eubanks.

It was during this contest that the Belfast roar was conceived. It wouldn't have a real life of its own until McGuigan got to the King's Hall, but even in embryonic form it was a force to be reckoned with. The battle with Eubanks was a ding-dong affair until McGuigan finally got on top in the sixth round through his superior strength. He was throwing every shot in the book at the man from Brighton when the referee heard what he thought was the bell. He separated the fighters and pointed them at their corners. When he realized his mistake it was too late. Eubanks had survived. His reprieve only lasted until the eighth round. This time McGuigan wanted to leave no doubt as to the outcome. He came forward relentlessly. The referee had no alternative but to stop the fight to prevent Eubanks taking any more punishment. The crowd went wild.

Less than a week later, McGuigan was in the Protestant church at the top of the Diamond, relatively unmarked, for his wedding to Sandra. Dermot, his brother, was the best man and the bridesmaid was a cousin of Sandra's, Gillian McMurray. After the ceremony the McGuigans, as the canon called them, headed down the steep steps of the Protestant church and around the corner into Fermanagh Street. A few hundred yards took them to the Catholic church on Church Hill where they had their own private little ceremony. A definition of ecumenical: worldwide, universal. Soon the McGuigans would be the most ecumenical couple ever to come out of Ireland.

PADDY THE IRISHMAN

After a one-sided points win against the Spaniard Luis La Sagra, McGuigan started stopping his opponents with a regularity that was frightening. Perhaps his strongest opponent in the first six months of 1982 was Angelo Licata, ranked number seven in Europe. In round two a white towel fluttered into the Ulster Hall ring. The man throwing it knew more than the crowd. McGuigan had destroyed his fighter's rib-cage, the way a power saw cuts down a tree. Every breath he took was like filling the burst balloon of his lungs with poison. Nobody could stay in the ring for more than three rounds with McGuigan without the threat of permanent damage to his health.

Before Barry and Sandra could make her a great-grand-mother, Mary McGuigan died. She had always remembered the early death of her eldest son, Dermot, but then she had the protection of youth to get her over the trauma. She had survived her husband, James, by almost fourteen years when her son Kevin died. Kevin was perhaps Barry's biggest fan. A carpenter by trade, he worked a lot with asbestos and there is no doubt that this contributed to his early death from cancer. Despite his unbounded energy and uncontrollable temper, Kevin had so often been sick in his last few years that nobody paid any particular attention when he fell ill in the early part of 1981. Within a couple of months he was dead. His mother did not survive him a year. After her funeral in 1982 Barry had only one surviving grandparent. McGuigan's dream had always been to come back to Clones to show them his world title. He was still three fights away from even a British title, and they were gone.

By now Barry had worked his way up the rankings of the British featherweight division. The only other challenger who ranked with him was Paul Huggins of Hastings. They would fight an eliminator, with the winner going on to meet Steve Sims for the title. Huggins was a non-stop action fighter, rough and ready, and a fight with him would fill the Ulster Hall to overflowing. There was just one slight problem in matching them for the eliminator: McGuigan was not a British citizen. Most of the other Irish fighters in the past qualified as British automatically because they were born in Northern Ireland or qualified as British subjects because they were born in the Republic before 1949. In that year the Irish Government withdrew the Republic from the Commonwealth, and if anybody from Southern Ireland wanted to fight for the British title he had to become a British citizen. The official communication from the British Boxing Board of Control confirmed this in their announcement of the Final Eliminator: 'This is subject to McGuigan becoming a naturalized British subject in accordance with Reg. 31, p. 4. The contest to take place in September.' Barry had four months to become a British subject. It had taken a lot of Irish people eight hundred years to go in the opposite direction. McGuigan knew his history well: his grandfather had been a member of the old Irish Republican Army.

All his life James McGuigan had been an Irishman first, a Northern Irishman second, and a British subject third. When Barry and Sandra first went out together, they would often visit Mary McShane who recounted her memories of the years in Donaghmore, Co. Tyrone. When the War of Independence broke out James McGuigan was arrested by the newly formed Black and Tans. It was the first phase of what later became known by the euphemistic term 'internment'. In essence, it was the mass jailing of a large part of the Catholic population of the largely Protestant Six Counties. James McGuigan was taken out of his house in the bottoms of his pyjamas and was led to a huge open-backed truck, the soldier in charge hitting him with the butt of a rifle to hurry his ascent; but there was no way he could do it, as his hands were tied behind his back. Mary's sister Margaret tried to intervene and the soldier put the bayonet of his rifle to her throat and told her to keep quiet or else. James McGuigan spent nine months in Ballykinlar Camp and, when he was finally released, Mary his wife hoped they could rebuild their fortunes which had declined as a result of his incarceration. Within a couple of months he was picked up again and he spent the next two and a half years in captivity on the prison ship the *Argenta* and in Magilligan Camp in Derry. Finally the RUC decided they would intern him no longer so they drove him to the border and, like Charlie Chaplin, they left him there. Penniless, with no future, James McGuigan followed the railway tracks into the nearest Southern Irish town. That town was Clones.

Although she may have felt it was an injustice, Mary McGuigan never bore any grudges that Sandra and Barry could see. Sandra Mealiff was her favourite visitor and she was delighted when Barry and Sandra announced their engagement. She never bore any grudge against Prot-estants. Protestants had their own crosses to bear. Sandra's cousins, the Eakins, live in Claudy, Co. Derry. In 1970 Sandra was on holiday with them. There was only a year or so in age difference between Sandra and Catherine so they were very close. On the Monday after they went home from their holiday, Catherine Eakin was dead. She was cleaning her mother's windows when a bomb went off at a garage close by. It broke her arm and cracked her skull. Mark, her brother, was standing close by at the time, but miraculously he was unhurt. He ran home past a crumpled body in the street. When he went out to look for his sister he went in the opposite direction to where Catherine lay. He didn't recognize her. She died on the way to hospital. When Sandra and Barry were married the bouquet went on her grave.

McGuigan knew enough by the age of fourteen to know that non-sectarianism would be a driving force in his life.

Every time McGuigan drives more than twenty miles from Clones in any direction, the road is littered with memories of innocent people who have died as a result of the troubles. McGuigan is a proud Irishman but he has an immense fear of sectarianism. 'I remember once at school there was a fight. It was a light-hearted affair. Suddenly one of the boys got hurt and he turned around and called the other boy a loyalist pig. Well, the temperature went up ten degrees in the next few seconds. It was frightening.' McGuigan will not be intimidated into taking sides. Every step McGuigan took retracing his grandfather's footsteps back into Northern Ireland was a courageous step of reconciliation.

When Pat McGuigan was asked, did McGuigan fight for Ireland or England, he replied that as an amateur Barry fought for his country and as a professional he fought for money. In his first year as a boxer he didn't earn very much. Sandra had opened a hairdressing salon with McGuigan's sister Sharon in May, but that wouldn't be a profitable venture for some time. The McGuigans went into debt banking on the future success of Barry as a boxer.

There was no structure for the professional game of boxing in the Republic of Ireland. Every Irish boxer who ever fought for the British title had taken out British citizenship: Spike McCormack and his sons, the gorgeous Gael Jack Doyle, Mick Leahy. McGuigan was different. He was a Catholic married to a Protestant who lived on the border. In the eyes of some people, taking out British citizenship was not just a question of bread and butter. It was a political stance. They saw it as the perfect opportunity for the British to exploit McGuigan. The only problem with this theory is that initially the British turned him down.

The application form had read like this: 'Registration of Commonwealth Citizens etc. as Citizens of the United Kingdom and Colonies'. People entitled to apply could be a citizen of any of the following countries:

Antigua and Barbuda, Australia, The Bahamas, Bangla-desh, Barbados, Belize, Botswana, Canada, Cyprus, Dominica, Fiji, The Gambia, Ghana, Grenada, Guyana, India, Jamaica, Kenya, Kiribati, Lesotho, Malawi, Malaysia, Malta, Mauritius, Nauru, New Zealand, Nigeria, Papua New Guinea, St Lucia, St Vincent and the Grenadines, Seychelles, Sierra Leone, Singapore, Solomon Islands, Sri Lanka, Swaziland, Tanzania, Tonga, Trinidad and Tobago, Tuvalu, Uganda, Vanuatu, Western Samoa, Zambia or Zimbabwe.

If you colour those countries a regal red in your mind's eye you get some idea of the extent of the Empire at one time. Still, Ireland wasn't there. It existed under a different heading which said simply 'or the Republic of Ireland'. Ireland's history was different from all the other do-minions. It was sadder and more painful. The necessary qualifications were a special relationship with Northern Ireland and five years' residence. McGuigan did have a special relationship with Northern Ireland. He had won a gold medal for them at the Commonwealth Games in Edmonton. He hadn't been resident the full five years, but it seemed impossible to Stephen Eastwood that they would turn down the application of someone who had driven seventy miles a day at his own expense as an amateur to fight for that country. Indeed it was part of the complexity of the relationship of Ireland and England that he should even have to apply, having fought for Northern Ireland already.

On 8 June 1982 a letter reached Eastwood House saying that as McGuigan did not fulfil the necessary requirement he could not be considered for citizenship. McGuigan as ever had to fight for everything he got. Many people who had seen Barry box and the effect it had in uniting the people of Belfast spoke up on his behalf. His greatest defender was Paddy Devlin himself, an avid boxing fan. 'Oh, I did all I could for Barry,' says Paddy. 'He doesn't allow any ill-will or hostility or triumphalism to flow from his victories. He's boxing for all of us. He's boxing for all the people of Ireland, all the people of Ulster and especially the people of Belfast. With him there's no feeling of superiority or inferiority, and everybody's behind him. We applied on the basis of his grandparents so that he could fight for the title.' The wheel had come full circle. James McGuigan was an Ulsterman, and Barry would qualify for British citizenship. On 1 August 1982 he finally got clearance. Maybe James McGuigan had not suffered for nothing after all. Everybody was happy. Only one man begrudged the action taken. His name was Paul Huggins.

THIS SPORTING LIFE

Meanwhile Barry had to go to London to fight the West African bantamweight champion Young Ali.

Close by the Grosvenor House Hotel in Park Lane there is a statue to an Irishman, Arthur Wellesley, Duke of Wellington. Achilles stands, an imposing figure, every part of his body down to his esteemed ankles cast from melted-down cannon used at various wars throughout the nineteenth century. On 6 June 1982 Barry McGuigan drove past Achilles, stopped at the door to the Grosvenor House Hotel and entered the lobby. Just inside on the left-hand-side wall is a painting commemorating one of the most auspicious occasions ever witnessed in the hotel. In it the painter is seated conveniently behind the Prince of Wales as he watches an ice-show. The skaters are dressed in motley and some are even dancing on stilts. The Prince appears to be having a good time. He and his entourage are smoking large cigars, and the rest of the company seem contented enough with the ice-show. The room in which all this is taking place is the Great Room. The Prince is seated on the lower balcony, surrounded by royalty. On the upper balcony sit the Lords, Ladies and Peers of the Realm.

The room as it stands today is almost the same as it was on that auspicious occasion in 1932 except that the lone chandelier has been replaced by no less than eight spectacular cousins that look like illuminated wedding dresses when the light is switched on. The floor in the centre of the room rises to make a natural arena.

This was not the Ulster Hall. This was fashionable London in June. The fight had been organized by the World Sporting Club. Membership of the Club was an honour. When the Club organized an event they did it well. The food matched the surroundings, which were first class. The atmosphere would be a thousand miles from that in the little Belfast hall. Displays of partisanship were frowned upon here. One did not cheer either one's champion or his opponent . . . that was not fair play. At the end of the round you clapped, depending on the level of expertise manifested by the two fighters.

It was a black-tie affair. As Barry came towards the ring he would have noticed more white coats than was normal at a fight. These were not stewards, however, they were waiters bringing drinks to the tables. Dinner had been served and now everybody was relaxing as the contests began. McGuigan got into the ring to a good round of applause. Young Ali came out. He only spoke a few words of English. He too got a round of applause. It must have spurred Ali on because that night he fought with the heart of a lion.

The bell rang for the first round. The fighters teased each other out. It is impossible to know what went through Young Ali's head that night. Here was a poor fighter from Africa in the most plush surroundings of his life, fighting a white man, watched by white men – and nobody was shouting McGuigan on. It must have had the quality of a dream. In the following rounds it would turn into a nightmare.

McGuigan for the first time in ages could actually hear what was going on in the other corner. In broken English Young Ali kept telling his corner, 'Too strong, too strong.' As if to indicate what he meant, he kept holding his gloves up to his jaw. The African's heart proved bigger and stronger than his body. In the fourth and fifth rounds McGuigan was surprised by the level of aggression Ali could mount. At the end of each round the knowledgeable crowd applauded enthusiastically. On the second balcony looking down, Alfie McLean, a life-long friend of Barney Eastwood, sat uncomfortably in his tuxedo. He felt sure he would be able to get out of it soon.

At the start of the sixth round McGuigan was amazed that Ali was still in there, considering the amount of punishment he had taken. Whether through resilience or tiredness, he had stopped protesting to his corner. McGuigan will never forget the sixth round. 'I hit him round the temples a lot. He was tired. The damage always occurs when a man is fatigued. I hit him with a punch right between the eyes. The eyes spun round in his head like the numbers on a slot machine. He fell. I stood back and he fell straight to the floor. I looked over at Mr Eastwood and he made a quick motion as if to say, "It's all over", but there was a worried look on his face. He pointed to a neutral corner and I went there, all the time looking at Young Ali.'

Up on the balcony the Belfast contingent were having a hard time behaving like gentlemen. Brian Eastwood turned to Big Alfie in euphoria. 'He'll never get up,' said Brian, not understanding the full import of what he was saying. Big Alfie was looking at the figure on the floor below him lying quiet and silent, the only motion disturbing the unnecessary count being that of the cigar smoke from a hundred private tables. Big Alfie repeated Brian's words and then added, 'That's right. He'll never get up. He's dead.'

Like McGuigan, Big Alfie underestimated the resilience of the bantamweight champion of West Africa. He rose to his feet with some assistance from his corner. McGuigan went to see how he was but was brusquely pushed away. Eastwood took him upstairs. The mood in the dressing room was sombre. Downstairs Young Ali was walking unassisted from the ring to warm applause. He fell a second time. This time he wouldn't get up. An ambulance was called. His cornermen improvised as best they knew how. They laid him out on one of the dining tables and wrapped a tablecloth around him for comfort. After about fifteen minutes he was carried from the Grosvenor House out into the night air and rushed to hospital. Sean Kilfeather was reporting another McGuigan victory back to his head office in Dublin when he heard an unusual sound. 'I heard this sound and I looked around and they were taking Young Ali

A PLAGUE
ON YOUR HOUSE

The only thing McGuigan could do was to carry on as if everything were normal. Young Ali was in a coma for six months. McGuigan couldn't think about the inevitable. His father, Pat, lifted some of the burden from his shoulders, ringing the hospital every night to see how Ali was faring. Every night the McGuigan family prayed that he would survive. Every detail of the fighter's personal background became known to McGuigan. He had a wife in Nigeria who was pregnant with his child.

McGuigan took to the hills, walking his dogs. To stop boxing now would be to admit that Young Ali would never recover. It was best to act as if nothing had happened.

Four months after the Ali fight, McGuigan was in the ring against Jimmy Duncan. Duncan boxed bravely. From deep down inside, McGuigan mustered all the aggression he could find. In the third round he threw a right and suddenly he was looking into the eyes of Young Ali. He stood mesmerized for a moment. McGuigan was fighting two opponents. One of them hit him an unmerciful punch. McGuigan retaliated and stopped Jimmy Duncan in the fourth round. It appeared as if he could never shake off the other.

Young Ali was flown home to Lagos. While the African lay in a hospital thousands of miles away, McGuigan faced a tough new opponent, Paul Huggins, in the Ulster Hall. The fight with Huggins was the most important so far of McGuigan's career. The winner would go on to fight for the British title. Huggins was a Rocky Marciano-style fighter, willing to absorb punishment to get inside to do his own damage. He was tough, aggressive and confident. McGuigan would need to be at the top of his form to beat him.

Huggins came forward relentlessly from the opening bell. McGuigan picked him off with every punch in the book. McGuigan wondered when the man from Hastings would learn his lesson and stop coming forward. He never did. McGuigan would have to teach him. In the fourth round McGuigan suddenly stopped still and fought Huggins inside, toe to toe. Usually that means that the boxers are just exchanging blows to see who has the greater strength. Not with McGuigan. He boxed brilliantly inside, hitting Huggins with everything and at the same time avoiding all the slugger's punches. Huggins was forced to step back. The next time he came forward McGuigan hit him with left jabs, right and left hooks. He even hit him with a punch he seldom uses, a lightning-fast uppercut. Huggins stood in the centre of the ring and shook his head as if to say, 'It doesn't hurt me.' Defiance was the only defence he had left. If boxing is a science, Huggins was being broken down into molecules of helplessness. In boxing you've got to use your head, but not the way Huggins did. It was as if he was using it as a magnet to attract McGuigan's best punches. With Huggins bleeding from the mouth, the referee stopped the fight at the end of the fifth round. McGuigan thanked God. All he could see as Huggins stood there shaking his head in defiance were the eyes of Ali.

One night after the McGuigan family had finished praying, Sandra came in to announce that she was pregnant. She and Barry would be expecting their first child in the middle of 1983. As everybody celebrated, McGuigan thought of the boy Young Ali's wife had given birth to. What would the child do if his father died? McGuigan shook the thought from his mind as he went out to look for a present for Sandra for their wedding anniversary. McGuigan would never forget his first wedding anniversary. It was the day that Young Ali died, far away.

McGuigan went into a fit of depression. He looked at his beloved Monaghan Hills with alienated eyes.

If a visitor from outer space came to Clones he might be forgiven for thinking that it was a plague town. In a deep arc about the town the small country lanes have been blocked with barriers that make passage impossible. Steel girders stick up from huge concrete slabs like metal fingers. One could be forgiven for thinking that it is the innocent-looking streams that carry the deadly virus. Like steps along a giant's pathway, bridges line the river bed. Human badgers have been at work clogging up the waterway.

McGuigan was about nine or ten when the plague started. At first it was just based in the city; slowly it spread to the countryside. Soldiers were sent to control it, but that only made things worse. Soon the atmosphere got more and more poisoned. One day it appeared on the streets of Clones. Cars seething with resentment exploded of their own volition. The drivers had been exposed to the plague and carried the deadly virus. Gradually, normality was reduced to a shambles. People resorted to desperate measures. Strangers became enemies. They pulled up the drawbridge and the traders around the town wondered what to do with their goods.

If you couldn't cure the plague, the best thing to do was to ignore it. One of the ways to do that was through sport. McGuigan boxed and he became so good that he boxed for his country. McGuigan had two countries; he boxed for both of them. Each country blamed the other for the plague. McGuigan blamed neither, he just fought. He won a gold medal for one country and then for the other. By an accident of birth and through his amazing boxing talent McGuigan had seen life from both sides of the border. People who hated each other would congratulate McGuigan after his victories. He, it seemed, was uncontaminated by the plague.

Ever since the start of the plague, McGuigan watched as his mother's business declined. The roads that are the arteries into Clones have become congealed and the town is suffering from a commercial heart attack. Shopping has become an ordeal. Whenever McGuigan meets a journalist or somebody who has never visited Ireland he will show them the border roads. He will jump into his jeep and head down towards the first army blockade. There is almost a sense of ritual about this, McGuigan has done it so often. He points out the army location, the bunkers hidden on the little hills of Fermanagh, the barricaded roads and the destroyed bridges. These crazy ruptures don't just threaten the trade of the little shop in Clones, they threaten a whole way of life. At a deep level of instinct, McGuigan is fighting to remove these barriers. Rather, he is fighting for a situation where the barriers won't be necessary. He's using his God-given strength to make a first tentative step to unblock these blood-clogged roads.

All situations reach a point where they won't be solved by logic. People need to stand back and judge the situation from a totally different perspective. With the death of Young Ali, McGuigan lost all sense of his own perspective.

In boxing, they say there is nowhere to hide in the ring. After the death of Young Ali, McGuigan had nowhere to hide, period. McGuigan felt as if a plague had been visited upon his own house. Boxing made things simple. It brought people together. Why then had God sent this tragedy to plague him personally? Every time McGuigan looked for an answer he was in a cul-de-sac. As McGuigan faced the new year he could find no reason to continue boxing. When he answered that he boxed for Sandra and the child she was pregnant with, he had to ask himself about Young Ali and the son who would never see his father. McGuigan decided to quit boxing. There was no other way out of his midwinter of the heart. Soon after New Year's Day in 1983 he journeyed to Belfast to tell Eastwood the bad news. Eastwood opened the door to him and said, 'No talking about boxing, do you hear me?' McGuigan sat there in silence and then returned home to Clones.

Two little thoughts kept McGuigan from announcing his retirement. What would it mean if he quit boxing now?

It would all have been for nothing. The training, the single-minded determination, the lost adolescence, the death of Ali, all for nothing.

And the press were fickle. Ali's memory wouldn't last beyond the next car bomb or plastic bullet. If McGuigan became world champion the people would never forget Alimi Mustapha. He would never allow them to forget. McGuigan decided that if he couldn't immortalize the African's name, then there was no point in fighting. He decided to come back and do just that. It meant he returned with an even fiercer determination than ever. Now when he got into the ring, the ghost of Ali would be standing behind him, urging him on. Every fighter lives with the presence of death. McGuigan had walked around like the old man of the sea with that demon on his back Now he had buried him deep inside. McGuigan looked through the eyes of death and he didn't blink.

AT HOME IN BELFAST

When McGuigan rang Eastwood to tell him he was coming back to fight, Eastwood immediately booked the King's Hall. The King's Hall is a huge exhibition space on the outskirts of Belfast. It holds over 7,000 people, but Eastwood was confident he could fill it with McGuigan fighting for the British title.

As McGuigan moved up the fight ladder his need for peace and quiet to help his concentration became more and more critical. Eastwood had found him the perfect training retreat in the seaside resort of Bangor. He and Buchanan could spend hours talking without interference.

One night when McGuigan was preparing for his fight for the British title, Buchanan rang Eastwood from Beresford House. 'I don't think he looks too well,' he said.

Eastwood suggested that he get to bed early, but Buchanan thought they should get him to a hospital. Soon McGuigan was in the Royal Victoria Hospital with a mysterious ailment. The events of the past few months had exerted a heavy toll. McGuigan lay limp and tired in the bed. The doctors said that he had a very severe flu and that it would be months before he could fight again. Eastwood had a dilemma: he had booked the King's Hall and McGuigan was the main attraction. McGuigan insisted he could recover.

Every night Eastwood turned up at the hospital with home-made soup, hoping that McGuigan would come round on time. Most of his problems were psychological, he reckoned. McGuigan agreed with him. One night he felt a little better. Eastwood was happy. He left the ward with McGuigan up on his feet pledging that he would get better.

That night Eastwood drove back to his new house on The Hill in Hollywood. The doctor was on the line from the hospital. McGuigan had got up out of his sick bed and started doing press-ups. He had had a relapse and he was now in a serious condition. McGuigan eventually recovered from his ordeal, but it showed the level of determination with which he was coming back to fight.

His fight for the British title eventually took place against Vernon Penprase on 12 April at the Ulster Hall. They could have sold out the smaller venue four times over. It was a fight – but no contest. McGuigan backed Penprase up with left jabs into a corner in the first round and then hit him with a lightning-fast left hook. Like a puppet whose strings have been cut Penprase fell to the floor. He had never been down in his life up to that moment but a thousand reputations couldn't have saved him from the accuracy of that punch. McGuigan came forward, saw his opportunity and let fly. Almost before the punch had landed he was facing towards a neutral corner. Penprase hauled on the ropes like a puppet whose horizontal and vertical strings have got all mixed up. He survived the round. In the second round McGuigan again pursued him and again caught him close to the ropes. A right hand sent him scuttling along the floor like a crab going sideways. He scrambled to his feet, his features lost in a cake of blood. The referee mercifully stopped the fight.

Sandra went to the hospital in Newry to get a scan on the baby. The McGuigans were amazed to see a fully formed baby appear under the conquering magic of ultrasound. The doctor could even tell the sex of the baby but the McGuigans said they didn't want to know; it would be like opening your present before Christmas. The doctor moved the sounding instruments close to the baby's heart. Sandra couldn't remember where she had heard that rhythmic beat before. The doctor moved on to other features of the baby, pointing them out to the expectant couple. Again the heartbeat came up and Sandra said, 'The Caribbean.' They had been there on their honeymoon. In the long echoing marble corridors of the hotel they were staying in, McGuigan had done his skipping religiously. The sound and tempo of the rope hitting the floor and causing the feedback of its own echo was an identical sound to the heartbeat of the baby.

After his victory in the British title fight McGuigan went on tour. His first fight took him south of the border to Navan in the Republic of Ireland. He was to meet Sammy Meck, who only a couple of months previously had fought a draw with Louis Stecca in the European championship, who went on to become Junior Flyweight Champion of the World. After the weigh-in McGuigan and Meck had a meal in the same restaurant. Eastwood remembers McGuigan's eyes lighting up at the amount of food Meck put away. 'The grub he ate you couldn't put in a five-gallon jar. He had two or three pints of stout and he ended up having ice-cream and he was smiling and laughing. Barry turned to me and said, "My God, he's going to get into the ring at least at nine stone ten." I turned to Barry and said, "He'll be ten stone nine." ' The meal didn't help Sammy. McGuigan beat him in six rounds in a very good fight. The referee stopped the fight in the sixth round after Meck took a hammering to the head and body from Barry's devastating left hook.

With the kind of foresight that sees problems before they arrive, Eastwood decided it was time to have a look at the United States. The first time most European boxers saw American opponents, they looked at them from a horizontal position. All the best trainers, coaches and managers were in the States, and most of the best fighters too.

Eastwood felt that McGuigan had gone as far as he could in Britain, and that it was time to lay the demons of the New World to rest. One of those demons, Loval McGowan, proved far less resilient than expected. He went down, and stayed there, in the first round. The real test came in the Chicago and New York gyms, where McGuigan soon became an unpopular sparring partner. Vinnie Costello's brother, Billy Costello, is a world champion, but that gave

Vinnie no right to be in the same ring as McGuigan, even in a spar. Vinnie was twenty pounds heavier than McGuigan, but he had to go on the retreat from the ferocity of McGuigan's punches. After the Costello spar, Costello's manager announced that 'McGuigan doesn't fight like a white man, he fights like a brother.'

In a corner, keeping to himself, was an old man, Bobby McQuillar. Eastwood asked him what he thought. 'Good, very good,' said McQuillar. Eastwood asked whether there was room for improvement. 'Sure,' said McQuillar. East-wood invited McQuillar to Belfast.

When McGuigan got home from the States, Sandra was almost eight months pregnant. On 24 August she began to go cabin crazy in their home, and asked Barry to take her for a meal. After the meal her waters broke. Barry drove her to the hospital in Newry. Everything went fine until the nuns offered her St Teresa's powder. As soon as she had taken it, Sandra began to feel sorry that she had had the meal. As the Catholic nuns looked at the effect the powder had had on her, McGuigan said, 'That's the Protestant blood in you.'

Soon after midday on 25 August 1983 their son was born. McGuigan was there at the birth. If you ask him why he boxes, he won't give you any of the reasons that make good copy for the press. 'Money and fame,' he will say. Sometimes there are limits. The press wanted a picture of Sandra and the new baby. McGuigan was about to tell them to come back another day when Sandra emerged, fresh and relaxed, ready to have her photo taken. Their son, Blain, was introduced to the wider world a few hours after his birth. Neither McGuigan nor Sandra wanted to call him after his father, and they decided on Blain, which is French for 'fair'. The child lived up to his name: he had a lovely head of fair hair.

The story of McGuigan's next two fights is the story of one punch, his left hook to the body. Delivered from below in an upward arc it hits to best effect just below the rib-cage, causing the opponent to search for breath and slowing him down as effectively as lead boots. McGuigan delivers with his weight on his left-hand side. Every athlete who dominates his time has one physical attribute that sets him apart from the rest. It's his special signature. It may not necessarily be his most effective action, but it is something that sets him apart in the public eye. Pelé had an overhead bicycling kick on his back so that you were trebly confused as to what angle the ball would take. Borg had his topspin which made the ball dip over the net as if it had hit an invisible wall just before you got to it. Lester Piggott rode so high in the saddle he looked as if he was coming down from a perpetual high jump. Perhaps the most famous signature of all was the Fosbury Flop, Dick Fosbury's backward leap over the bar that looked so extraordinary when he introduced it but is now the staple leap in high jump competitions. McGuigan's left hook to the body has always been there in boxing but, because of McGuigan's strength, it is an awesome weapon for a featherweight; and because of the size of target he has to aim at, it is very difficult to neutralize. When McGuigan first used it against his early opponents, it almost doubled them in two. The only defence – apart from running – is to bend really low and bring the arms down close to the body. The result of this is that McGuigan has often been cautioned for low blows.

Ruben Herasme fought well in his first round with McGuigan, then he felt the full weight of McGuigan's left hook. The first thing Herasme registered was the pain and then the urge to get away from it as quickly as possible. In the second round another left hook to the body slowed him down. This left him open to the full McGuigan arsenal: left hook to the chin, right to the head and finally the devastating left hook to the body again. The man from the Dominican Republic went down and then spat out his gumshield in a gesture that said, 'That's it, I've had enough.'

Valerio Nati had more to fight for: the vacant European featherweight title. This was McGuigan's first fight in the

King's Hall. The Belfast crowd knew they were watching history being made. The sound they made rolled like thunder round the huge dome of the hall. To McGuigan it was worth an extra arm. Nati stumbled round the stadium like Lear in the storm. By the third round he felt as old as the Celtic patriarch. Between rounds he stood in his corner. The reason for this was that he couldn't sit down: he had suffered three broken ribs. He was a durable fighter. He stayed on his feet until the sixth round when McGuigan caught him with a couple of left hooks to the body. Nati ran for cover but couldn't find any. Most fighters go down because they have lost control of their legs. Nati's legs were still intact but his body was in ruins. He doubled up in a corner, cowering from McGuigan's body shots like a dog avoiding an irate master. It was an end that didn't do any kind of justice to the extraordinary courage he had shown.

The Belfast fight crowd are very knowledgeable. They cheered Nati in defeat. High up in the King's Hall somebody banged out a rhythm on a lambeg drum that signified the best European victory since the Battle of the Boyne. This time Catholics and Protestants were united in victory. The people of Belfast had something to cheer at last. Muhammad Ali articulated the dumb soul of black America. A voice that had been kept in thrall suddenly broke out in the words and fists of Ali. The Irish nationalist and loyalist causes had been overarticulated to the point of exhaustion. The people didn't need somebody who boasted what he was going to do, they needed a hero who did more than he said. McGuigan was one of the first of the television generation who believed more in what they saw than in what they heard. That night he saw over 7,000 people release a scream in tears of deep emotion that drowned out the frustration they had felt for years.

McGuigan has some idea of his appeal: 'In the ring, I'm their hope, their little bit of prosperity. The frustration at what Northern Ireland has become, on fight nights they let it all out. They love me. I feel so responsible for those people. I'd hate to let them down, not because I'm afraid of them. They're genuine people. They would sell their houses to go and see me. I love Belfast. Put the troubles aside, the people of Belfast are great people. That's my story. That's it in a nutshell.'

A CONTENDER

McGuigan came to Jean Anderson's guest house in Bangor just after Christmas in 1983, more determined than ever to work his way to the top. And work he did. He was like a greyhound in the gym. Eastwood and Eddie Shaw had never seen him in better condition. For his fight with Charm Chiteule of Zambia he sparred 130 immaculate rounds. Then in the King's Hall on 25 January for five rounds it looked as if he had left it all in the gym. Chiteule was a seasoned campaigner, a thorough professional. While McGuigan was warming up, Chiteule was scoring repeatedly, getting through McGuigan's defence straight to the head. By the third round one of McGuigan's eyes was swollen and by the fifth he had problems with his vision. Every time McGuigan tried to get inside, the Zambian was picking him off. McGuigan wiped his gloves on his trunks in the sixth round and brought his performance up a notch. Champions win when they are not performing well. To pull it out from where he was at the start of the sixth, McGuigan would need to be a real champion. His body punches were neutralized to the extent that he had been warned for punching low. He looked at the referee with his one good eye. It was the same man who had given the decision against him in the Peter Eubanks fight. He had to stop Chiteule. Gradually he adapted to the range that he needed for one eye. Slowly he began to get inside Chiteule and the Zambian weakened. After a barrage of punches in the tenth round the referee stopped the fight. Chiteule stood stock still in the corner into which McGuigan had driven him. It was McGuigan's toughest match to date. He would need to improve for his next fight against Jose Caba.

Jose Caba had gone fifteen rounds with the great Eusebio Pedroza in his last fight, but Eastwood reckoned that McGuigan could take him out. McGuigan fundamentally trusts Eastwood's judgement in such matters. Eastwood reckoned Caba was ripe for the taking. He had just lost the most important fight of his life against Pedroza, a big psychological blow. That fight was a real battle and Caba came out of it a wiser if sadder man.

Fighters from the United States generally regard European opposition with affection. Most of the Europeans fight a very upright fight, leaving themselves a big target for the ultra-professional Americans. Caba couldn't believe what he saw in the King's Hall. The noise the crowd let loose made his fight with Pedroza seem like an altercation in a pool hall. McGuigan fought like a man possessed. Caba could not land a blow. He had come to protect himself from McGuigan's heralded body shots but McGuigan hardly threw one all night. Instead he caught him to the head with the most flawless exhibition of boxing ever seen in Belfast. Caba's squat coming-forward style was made for McGuigan and he tore him apart. The referee stopped the fight in the seventh round.

The fight against Caba shot McGuigan up the world ratings. In some quarters he was rated as high as number four.

A few days before McGuigan's defence of his European title against Esteban Equia of Spain, Eastwood found himself in a dilemma. The fight was at the Albert Hall in London. Equia would carry the Spanish flag into the ring. Mickey Duff, the English fight promoter in association with Stephen Eastwood, wanted McGuigan to carry the Union Jack into the ring. McGuigan had walked a tightrope with the fight fans in Belfast, never alienating one side or the other. In England the Union Jack is a flag of identity. In Ulster for sixty per cent of the population it is a flag of identity and a flag of defiance. McGuigan had refused to alienate the Protestants of Belfast by carrying the Tricolour. He would alienate the Catholics by carrying the Union Jack.

Eastwood asked McGuigan what he thought. McGuigan did not want to alienate anybody. 'I'm for peace,' he told Eastwood. 'Right then,' said Eastwood, 'we'll carry a peace flag.' He and Paddy Byrne set off across London to find it. A shop-owner showed them the flags of every nationality, but he had never heard of a peace flag. 'What does it look like?' he asked Paddy Byrne. 'It's got a dove on it,' said Paddy in his best Dublin accent. The flag man looked at Paddy as if he had two heads. He had never seen a flag with a dove on it anywhere in his life. The Japanese one was a little odd with its round moon, but he had been fifty years in the flag business and he had never seen one with a dove on it. They went back to the Holiday Inn where they were staying and considered the possibility of making a flag. In the bar one man who had had a few too many started to draw what he swore was the peace flag. The manager of the hotel happened to be passing and he overheard the conversation. 'We have a peace flag,' he said, 'outside the hotel, hanging up.' They went outside and there was the only peace flag to be found in London. That decided the issue. They were fated to carry the flag of peace. They got it down off the pole and carried it to the Royal Albert Hall.

The fight itself was anything but peaceful. McGuigan had progressed to a level far beyond the usual European standard. Equia was totally outclassed. In the same hall in which his father had sung in the Eurovision Song Contest, McGuigan knocked the Spaniard out in the third round.

Now the American TV networks wanted McGuigan. He is the type of boxer the American public love: aggressive, coming forward all the time, and with a knockout punch that makes him entirely unpredictable. He also has an intense personality, good looks, and is articulate. Who could ask for more? During McGuigan's first fight on American TV, the commentators couldn't believe the atmosphere in the King's Hall. Their equipment wasn't built to cope with that level of noise. His opponent, Paul De Vorce, was rated in the top twenty in the world, but after five rounds the referee had to step between the fighters as the man from Yonkers had stopped fighting back. The Americans thought the referee had stopped it too early. They couldn't get enough of McGuigan. De Vorce had had too much.

McGuigan's next opponent, in October 1984, was a late stand-in, the six-foot-tall Filipe Orozco. McGuigan brought him down with repeated shots to the body and then a huge left hook that sent the Colombian sprawling to the canvas.

McGuigan now had to defend his British and European titles against Clyde Ruan. If Ruan could beat McGuigan, he would suddenly be catapulted into the world rankings. He tried to intimidate McGuigan with talk ... he would finish off the job his friend Chiteule had started. In the gym at the bottom of the Falls Road, McGuigan prepared in silence. Four days before the fight, just after his wedding anniversary, McGuigan was dealt a double blow. His grandfather, 'Papa' Rooney, died. McGuigan had always been close to Katie's father. He helped out in the shop and his common-sense advice was one of the bedrocks on which McGuigan had built his career. At the same time as his grandfather died, Sandra had a miscarriage. McGuigan had to reach deep down to stop this double tragedy affecting him. The man who got the brunt of his temper was Clyde Ruan. He hit McGuigan with his best shot, a left to the head. McGuigan didn't blink. After toying with Ruan for three rounds, McGuigan knocked him out with a spectacular left hook to the jaw.

By now a theory was abroad in Belfast that McGuigan was an Eastwood creation and that he would fold up against a top-class opponent. According to this theory, anybody of world stature that McGuigan had beaten was already washed up. It is true that Eastwood had looked after McGuigan spectacularly well; they prepared for each fight on its merits, getting in the best and most appropriate sparring partners and devising the best tactics. The theory would be tested once and for all by Juan Laporte of Puerto Rico. Laporte was only twenty-six and had been world champion only a year previously. He had gone the distance with the great Eusebio Pedroza. Here was real opposition at last. Most importantly, Laporte had a deadly punch.

A short right hand from Laporte in the fifth caught McGuigan flush on the jaw. McGuigan was rocked. He hung on for a second and then, for the first time in the fight, boxed on the retreat . . . but for a few seconds he had looked really vulnerable. For four more rounds, Laporte looked for a way to perfect that right he had thrown in the fifth. He had no other alternative; McGuigan was fighting like a waterfall, constantly coming forward, weaving and ducking. In the ninth round he came forward – with his guard down. Laporte saw his chance. This is what he had been loading up for all night. He caught McGuigan with a long right hand to the jaw. McGuigan's left foot left the canvas perpendicularly. It was a copybook shot. McGuigan shook his head and then came forward again. The fight was over. He had shown that he could take a sledge-hammer of a punch. Eastwood had said that McGuigan was like a classic horse who had never been off the bit. Against Laporte we saw a little of what he looked like when given a free rein. He would need to fight better than that to beat Pedroza.

Eastwood went to Panama to get the world champion to sign for the title fight, and came back empty-handed. The problem was a man called Santiago del Rio. He was Pedroza's manager and he was the toughest negotiator Eastwood had ever met. On 26 March, McGuigan was due to defend his European title against a Frenchman, Farid Gallouze, at the Wembley Arena in London. Pedroza and his manager were talked into coming over to negotiate a world title fight, but on the night of the Gallouze fight the Master of Ceremonies announced that Pedroza had a head cold and couldn't attend. The psychological battle had begun. Finally, at six o'clock on the morning after McGuigan's two-round victory, Pedroza signed a contract for the most expensive featherweight title fight ever to be staged in Britain. McGuigan packed his bags. Into a corner he put his medals and the lucky charm an Indian had given him out of the blue. McGuigan headed home to Clones to prepare for the biggest night of his life.

Part Four

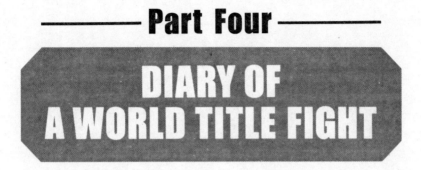

DIARY OF
A WORLD TITLE FIGHT

About McGuigan there is always the feeling of forward motion. There is very little distance between the decision and the deed. There is no orange light, no flashing 'Get ready' signal. There are so many people who will say 'I won't wait' that the fun is in the amount of leeway in the statement. They'll dilly and dally and so do you, working out some comfortable relationship in the drama in which you have been cast together. McGuigan never makes statements like that, he just puts his foot on the accelerator. Today we are driving to Bangor.

There are no crowds to wish us goodbye. It's as if McGuigan wants to leave with the minimum of fuss. Today he goes off to fight the champion of the world. To make a fuss would give Pedroza a stature that McGuigan can never allow him to attain. This is what his father calls Barry's gunshot vision. He never lets the target out of his mind. For the next four weeks the target is Pedroza and Barry's vision is trained on him; but his sights are telescopic and for the moment Pedroza is in long shot. When he wants, Barry can zoom him into focus, but only when he wants to illuminate some blemish in the Panamanian's make-up. I have been with Barry day and night for months now, and I have never heard him discuss Pedroza in public. Dermot watches the videos and analyses the faults. Barry concentrates on what Barry can do. You know that nobody can really help . . . that between McGuigan and Pedroza, it's a private affair. For Barry watching videos of Pedroza is like watching a home movie of a former wife where, while looking for faults to ease the pain of alimony payments, all you can see are her virtues.

143

McGuigan as ever drives too fast, especially on the road to Monaghan, which in the high suspension of his shōgun jeep feels as if it was built for the ass and cart. These are the kind of roads that would give you false teeth. Even blindfolded now I could tell the South from the North. And without looking I can tell when we cross the border because there are two huge bumps, camel style, to impede access to those who can separate bricks from mortar with the push of a button. I wonder, did any poor unfortunate ever cross these paths blindfolded, and then I wonder, does everybody cross these roads blindfolded?

Fifty yards inside the border at Middletown we are met by the biggest detachment of British soldiers I have seen in the past few weeks. These men could have been set down anywhere in the world and they would take up the same crouching positions. They hug the kerbside for protection, the way an old dog hugs a turf fire. With their blackened faces they look like extras from a film, but the guns are real ... the guns are real. With a look of recognition that is too wary to be a smile, the sergeant in charge waves us on and we drive towards the city of Armagh in silence.

We have passed many McGuigan landmarks on the way and nothing has been said about them: the spot where his father crashed, his first club in Smithboro, Mulligan's house, the town where he was born, all have passed in silence. Suddenly on the motorway outside Armagh, McGuigan points out a house and says, 'The fellow that lives in there is a great guy. His wife was abducted. They just walked in, in the middle of the day, and took her away. They were after a ransom. Lucky for her she escaped.' I note that there doesn't seem to be any extra protection on the house and McGuigan answers with the resignation of one who knows, 'Sure, what can you do?'

As we skirt Belfast, McGuigan repeats the phrase that is almost a catch-cry every time the city is mentioned: 'Great city, great people.' We drive on for a few miles until we are on a steep incline and the sea in its evening silver gown makes a majestic entrance, only to disappear as quickly behind an impudence of concrete. For a couple of hundred yards it enters and exits between rows of houses with the speed of the maid in a French farce. Eventually we pull up at the back of a four-storey house. We go into the kitchen, there is nobody about. There is no mistaking the two men out front. They sit on the front porch looking out at the Irish Sea. We approach and they greet us with the only word of English they know: 'McGuigan.' Barry nods. Eventually Jean Anderson appears and lays out a meal. It's not known if the Panamanians are hungry and eventually it is established that they are in fact starving. What do they want to eat? Now everybody is in on the pantomime. 'What is it? Fish? Eggs? Do they want pineapples or something?' Jose resolves the dilemma by squatting down, spreading his elbows out from the sides and squawking. 'Chicken,' says Barry as he erupts in laughter.

We take a walk down to the sea. On our walk we see a sign which tells us that the French National Circus are performing at the Castle Grounds until the 18th. The harbour is well laid out. Bangor is a seaside resort. The sea is faintly hinting at its elemental power. I walk a narrow strip that serves as a landing for small craft. 'I don't like the sea,' says Barry. I look surprised. 'I'm afraid of it,' he says. Fear is not a word I associate with McGuigan.

TUESDAY
14th May

First day in the gym. The Panamanians turn out to be Jose Marmalejo and Ezekiel Muskera. The cool one is Ezekiel: he watches the road into Belfast with an amused indifference. Jose holds on to his piece of Panama with the blaring Latin sounds from his Walkman. We pass a barbed-wire army encampment and a helicopter shoots out from the trees like a surprised iron bird. The words 'First Border Regiment' flash by and if you are going slowly enough to catch anything else you're on a bicycle. We pass a football stadium, well decorated in graffiti. On the side of the stand a gin bottle pours a perpetual liquid that turns into a silver cordial in strong sunlight. It possesses an other-world charm. When first erected it must have had the brashness of neon.

On our right ahead loom two fifty-foot iron goalposts emblazoned with the initials of their owners. HW. This is Harland and Wolff. This is the yard that built the *Titanic*. From here a largely Protestant workforce marched like an army all through the hungry Thirties and Forties to their homes. These were the hard men of the North. At school I learned that the reason the *Titanic* sank was because they had given it the number, NO. 909E. When you hold that up to a mirror it says NO POPE. In Catholic retribution God turned a portion of the North Atlantic into iced water and the demonic intentions of the Protestants were sunk with all hands on deck. We pass other monuments to the Protestant work ethic. Short Bros, the Sirocco Works. Within a half-mile we are crossing Bridge End and heading for Eastwood House.

It's only much later that I realize our journey to Chapel Lane performs bypass surgery around the heart of Belfast. The centre of the city is City Hall and on any map issued after 1975 the streets within a quarter-mile semicircle due north of it are coloured a deep red. The legend will tell you 'limited access'. This is the bleeding heart of Belfast.

At the outer perimeter of this half-circle where the red arteries turn white, Chapel Lane meets Castle Street. A casual passer-by might be forgiven for thinking that this is the Grand Central Station of Belfast. Taxis leave this junction at the rate of five a minute. This is the Belfast black taxi service that feeds the Catholic Falls. A hundred yards away another feeds the Protestant Shankill. They replaced the normal buses that were discontinued at the height of the troubles and are the tip of the iceberg of an alternative economy that grew up around the troubles. The Eastwood gym is at the bottom of the Falls Road, but it doesn't matter which taxi you take, you'll get into the workshop without being asked your religion. All you'll be asked is, 'Can you defend yourself within the Marquess of Queensberry rules?'

The posters in Bangor gave the wrong location for the Circus. It's here in Chapel Lane. There are three or four television crews, a dozen cameramen, a reporter for every cameraman and a friend for every reporter. The only shade from the hot glare of the television lamps is the fog of smoke that ascends from the mouths of all the non-sportsmen in the room. The man who is responsible for these overcast conditions enters the gym with his usual walk that says 'I'm going somewhere'. This time it's straight to the changing room at the bottom of the room. There he sits for a moment and considers the interest he has created and the hope he has awakened. There are some familiar faces around who can help get the work in perspective. Eddie Shaw is there. Eddie is a rock. He just gets on with the business. This won't faze Eddie. McGuigan strips and gets ready. He will spar with Jose and Ezekiel. When Jose gets into his gear his name is emblazoned all over it: 'Marmalejo' on the back and 'Jose' on the pants. No mistaking this man in a crowd. It's only then that I realize that McGuigan has no personalized items apart from the gown he steps through the ring in.

Eddie has assembled his bits and pieces on a trolley at the far end of the ring nearest the changing room. The adhesive tape hangs from the top deck where a large basin holds a few floating gumshields. On the lower deck there is olive oil and vaseline. Eddie applies the vaseline to Barry and Ezekiel with a deftness that belongs more to the theatre than the boxing ring. It gives McGuigan's face an odd sheen, almost as if Eddie were moulding him for a bust. The purifying fire will come in the ring. McGuigan warms

147

up. Most boxers do this by throwing shapes. It's a kind of performance before the main event, like a prima donna clearing her vocal cords, but with McGuigan you never get the feeling that it is a performance. He is not throwing blows at an imaginary opponent. It's as if he's throwing punches at himself and listening for the response his body makes.

For the first time since I met him, Barry is wearing a protective helmet. Ezekiel is about 21 pounds heavier than McGuigan and he never loses his cool. Because he never loses his cool he keeps on the move from McGuigan's blows, hugging the ropes with the speed and tenacity of a car on the Wall of Death. And when he moves inside he has the uppercut that Pedroza has perfected. It's not just the result of a conscious style, this is the method that best suits the fluidity of the Panamanians' make-up, physically and emotionally. It was something of a scoop for Eastwood to get these two Panamanians and there is a glint in those genial eyes when he is asked what effect it will have on Pedroza when he hears that two of his fellow countrymen are helping McGuigan out. Round one to Eastwood. After two rounds with Ezekiel, Jose jumps through the ropes. His style is a variation on a common denominator whose name is Muhammad Ali. The same rapid flow movement, stop, attack, retreat and flamboyance. Suddenly McGuigan hits him with a weapon from the arsenal. Jose lets out a piercing wail that is a coded war-whoop and stands toe to toe with McGuigan, centre ring, blows landing from every angle, the long wail punctuated with the thud of padded gloves. Eastwood and Eddie are delighted at McGuigan's condition. They are delighted that he is not too sharp, there is something to work on. He has been telling the truth. He has not been sparring at home. The press love Jose's performance and when he quits the ring after two rounds he keeps up the act on the overhead ball, only he hits the bag with his elbows. The press turn their arc-lamps on Jose and all eyes turn to the little platform underneath the speedball. Cameras flash. Alone in the ring, fighting his own particular shadow, McGuigan takes all this in. The media's eyes are as quicksilver and fickle as those of the magpie.

WEDNESDAY
15th May

Today is election day in Belfast. It is not the elections to the mother parliament in the United Kingdom, but the elections that control all the little local and urban councils, the ones that control sanitation and water rates rather than defence and the umbilical link across the Irish Sea. In the gym it's work as usual. Since coming to Belfast, Barry has been constantly in demand by the media, and the cracks are beginning to show. He tells a journalist from a Southern Irish paper that the dressing room is private which, given the evenness of Barry's temperament, is a major gaffe. Eastwood is busy keeping everybody happy. He has promised Barry that all the press will stop on Monday the 20th. It's different from when Eastwood started the boxing in Belfast. Then he had to go looking for stories to try and fill the Ulster Hall.

George Ace is the journalist closest to Eastwood. 'When Eastwood rang me to tell me he had got McGuigan, I said we need boxing here in Belfast like we need a hole in the head. Belfast was a dead city at night. The city centre was deserted.'

After training, Eastwood is in the Hercules bar across the road from the gym. The local journalists who have followed Barry since his first professional fight are feeling that their territory is being invaded by the Fleet Street hordes, not to mention 'women' journalists from *Newsweek* and *The New York Times* who have not a clue about boxing. McGuigan is becoming before their very eyes that most

149

hated of journalistic clichés, 'a human interest story'. Their fears and paranoias are focused on where they will actually sit at the fight and whether in fact they have been allotted seats at the ringside. Eastwood leans forward with his elbow on the bar and his upper body bent at the most obtuse angle to the company. He has a talent for making public utterances sound like boudoir stories. 'There will be tickets for all you lads. See, if the Queen of England and King Kong were sitting there, it's get them out of here and let these boys in. That's the story. There will be tickets for everybody.' Eastwood might flirt with the international press, but he knows he has to live with these boys. 'Do you remember the first time I had a press conference to announce McGuigan?' Eastwood asks philosophically. 'People said, "You're wasting your time. Boxing is dead here. Why don't you let it sleep? You're living twenty years ago. You won't fill half the hall. McGuigan is not even a local boy." I went down that road that night talking to myself.'

THURSDAY
16th May

By now Barry has settled into some sort of a routine. Most mornings he gets up around half-past eight and goes for a five-mile run. Then it's back to the Beresford for breakfast, which usually consists of All-Bran, some prunes, orange juice and coffee. Then it's back to bed in room seven. Barry chose this room because seven is a lucky number for him, and the fact that it doesn't look out on the seafront is a decided advantage. There are no distractions, not even the Irish Sea and Bangor Harbour. I reckon Barry spends twelve to fourteen hours a day in this room in total isolation. He doesn't sleep all the time. Some of the time he just lies there and thinks. The only thing he can think about clearly is the upcoming fight with Pedroza. He spends from eleven until one or two o'clock in his little bedroom. Then he packs for the gym and heads off. He arrives at the gym usually about three o'clock, spends about thirty to forty-five minutes getting ready. Between sparring and other workouts he usually does the equivalent of eighteen rounds until five o'clock, when he heads back to Bangor for dinner at seven. After dinner he walks between two and four miles and then it's back to bed and up again at half-past eight the next morning for more of the same. That he can keep an even temperament while doing this mind-boggling routine is extraordinary. This week he has the added pressure of the media. The only break from the routine is the nightly phone-call to Sandra. He will discuss how things went and what's happening in Clones. I knew that he trained every day in Clones, but there he would train at different times and in different ways. Here the punishment is constantly the same. It seems that he has reduced the outside world to a point where it has little or no effect on him. He concentrates like a Buddhist on the task ahead. It's as if he is storing energy, but it takes an immense inner calm to be able to store that energy without demanding release in any form. The evening walks seem to be designed to wear off the effects of dinner. He never stops and chats or lets his attention wander for longer than a few seconds. Then it's back to the room and Mr Wall. Some nights I know he doesn't sleep till three or four in the morning, and all the time he is thinking about the contest ahead. The contest he seems to be having now is with himself. He seems to be gaining total control of his environment and himself and forcing all his concentration towards one explosive hour in London in three and a half weeks.

By Thursday Ezekiel and Jose, in a joint effort to counter-act McGuigan's strength, are urging each other on. Ezekiel is shouting. The word he uses means 'toes' in English and it doesn't need elaboration. Jose renders Barry immobile by standing on them. Inside he pulls him to the floor and both he and Ezekiel constantly use the uppercut . . . what Pedroza's camp call his bolo punch. Boxing depends a lot on hand–eye co-ordination. A boxer's reflexes are like a wireless that shifts its setting until it picks up the particular wavelength of the opponent. The wavelength Barry is picking up this week is as foreign as the Spanish the Panamanians speak. It needs constant fine tuning to adjust and then a complete shift from one wavelength to another as something new crops up. Once the opponent's technique becomes familiar it loses a lot of its terror.

Each night and early morning, McGuigan plays over in his mind the sparring of the previous day. In one simple move to block Pedroza's bolo and left hook there were twelve separate moves before he could get in his own left hook to the body. Twelve different physical actions in two seconds, and then if the combination changes you must be ready to adapt. That would blow a fuse in a computer. McGuigan is training to adapt and paying dearly for the privilege. He shows me the underpart of his chin where the Panamanians have repeatedly caught him with uppercuts over the past three days. There are many small scars and welts, but the day he shows it to me is the day he has the problem licked. From that day on, I could count on one hand the number of times he's caught by the uppercut. That's the way McGuigan works.

On Thursday Eddie is happier. With the kind of tri-umphant sarcasm that is peculiar to boxing he tells Barry that Jose is '. . . eating that left. He's eating it.' Eastwood is leaning over the ropes whispering encouragement. 'One up, two down. You see, this Pedroza if you catch him with one of a combination you'll not catch him with two. If you hit him once to the head switch to the body.' Eastwood has the eyes of a child. He sees things simply. He has the tongue of a hundred-year-old yogi. He rarely speaks above a whisper so that you lean forward to hear what he has to say and if he raises his voice he's in a temper. I noticed, all the time we were in Clones, McGuigan looking to the mirror to get confirmation or inspiration. Outside of Clones, Eastwood is his mirror. Today, Eastwood is happy enough. 'No sparring tomorrow, that's enough for the time being, we'll just work out tomorrow, give the boys a day off.'

Today the election results start to come in. The Unionist Party have regained the lead as the majority Protestant party, relegating the Reverend Ian Paisley's Democratic Unionist Party to second place. On the Catholic side the vote is split almost fifty-fifty between the moderate SDLP and Sinn Fein who are the political wing of the Provisional IRA. Nobody in the gym or around it has mentioned elections or politics since the day we arrived. Today Barry is not sparring and while he and Eddie walk round the ring like Mowgli and Baloo in *The Jungle Book*, it's time to look round the gym. It's a complete contrast to the one in Clones. Everything is custom-built and, unlike most gyms throughout the world, it is spotlessly clean. It is about fifty feet in length with a large window stretching across its twenty-foot width at the Castle Street end. There are three heavy bags at this end and a speedball. From the windows all the way down to the ring are photos and mementoes. It's an indication of how long Eddie Shaw has been around that there is a framed picture programme from the time he was on the same bill as Sonny Liston in the early Sixties.

Elsewhere there is a picture of the last time big-time boxing hit Belfast. In it Freddie Gilroy and Johnny Caldwell stride through Belfast with a gait that tells us that these boys owned the city. Their fight at the King's Hall in October 1962 is part of Belfast folklore. Although they were from different sides of the religious divide, the bout was

153

unmarked by any form of sectarianism. Boxing's history in this regard is a proud one.

The ring itself is the one that the last undisputed Irish world flyweight champion, Rinty Monaghan, used for training. Barry was one of the last people who visited Rinty in hospital just before he died of cancer in 1984.

Over the next few weeks I will watch the pictures on the wall come alive. That night in the Hercules I see a face at the end of the bar. 'That's Johnny Caldwell,' says George Ace. Eventually we are introduced and Johnny almost pulls the hand off me with a handshake that still carries some of the power he took with him into the ring. Asked who he thinks will win, Johnny says he doesn't know, he has never seen Pedroza box, but he says, 'That McGuigan is a bad quilt,' which is Belfast slang for destroyer. Perhaps behind Johnny's reticence on Pedroza is the fact that when he boxed for the undisputed bantamweight title of the world, he came up against Eder Jofre, one of the great fighters of all time. Maybe at the back of his mind is the fact that Pedroza might be in that league. That would put paid to speculation as to whether Pedroza is over the hill because of his age. It is unimportant whether Pedroza is twenty-nine or thirty-two when one considers that Jofre won the title back at the age of thirty-seven.

On the way back to Bangor we have to go round Belfast because of a bomb scare. Although there is an army presence everywhere, the city is much improved from the nightmare of the early Seventies. Even at the barricade outside the door of the gym in Castle Street, people are rarely stopped. Spot searches are conducted, but the reality of the situation is that there hasn't been a bomb in the centre of Belfast in two years.

We are sitting in the Beresford, waiting on Ray the driver to take us to the gym, when in the distance we hear the sound of a marching band. It's a beautiful Saturday and the seafront at Bangor is lined with weekend tourists. As the crowd look up Grays Hill we can hear the approaching thunder of lambegs. Not since the old Corpus Christi processions have I seen such spectacle and colour. As flamboyant as a Spanish feast-day in Guatemala, the banners march down the steep hill towards the sea. Bibles, crowns and keys are the chief emblems on the banners which are carried fluttering along Queens Parade at the seafront. Most enigmatic of all is what looks like a musketeer on a horse. This is the legendary King William of Orange, defender of the Protestant faith. These are the insignia of true-blue northern Protestantism. The crown spells loyalty, although the man on the horse was a Dutchman who overthrew the Catholic King of England. The melody is carried in delicate high notes by an abundance of tin whistles and flutes and the rhythm is banged out on side drums and the huge lambegs. This is a parade of young schools, so the lambegs are carried by the older, stronger pupils. The parade itself is marshalled by the elders who are dressed in the main in suits and bowler hats with the orange sash draped over their shoulders. Most carry umbrellas which sometimes double as stewarding instruments. The parade takes us on a tour of Bangor.

In most northern towns the Catholic and Protestant steeples battle to dominate the skyline like actors trying to upstage one another. In Bangor both the steeples are of the Protestant denomination. The parade mounts Main Street. At the top of the street it turns abruptly away from the first Presbyterian church, one of the oldest in Bangor, and continues down Dufferin Street past St Comghalls Parish

Church and past the Masonic Hall. The parade comes to a halt outside Dufferin Hall and the boys in an orderly fashion divest themselves of their instruments and lodge them in the hall. The True Blues of Portadown are still holding the fort outside as boys in cockaded hats re-emerge into the sunlight. The boys head down to the seafront to get hamburgers and chips and the ones carrying the lambegs head to watering holes to relieve their thirsts. One chap has his lambeg belt undone and his name inscribed on the inside: 'Dutch'.

The RUC have nothing to fear from this parade. In their armoured cars at the seafront they sit eating pink ice-cream cones as they wait for their pizza to cook. At home in Beresford House, McGuigan sits in his room, unmoved by the spectacle. The parade could have come through the house itself and I don't think McGuigan would have noticed.

SATURDAY NIGHT

The little walkabout has stimulated some interest in Bangor. Like most Irish towns it had a religious beginning. It was in Bangor that St Comghall built his monastery. The offices of the order are recorded in the Antiphonary of Bangor. The regime of the enclosed monastic order was one of the toughest in the British Isles; it would have suited McGuigan down to a 't'. It's only in the dedication of those early Christians that I can think of a parallel with the man in room seven staring at the wall. This man has been fighting since he was eleven, and for the last ten years he has had his mind bent on becoming champion of the world. His dedication has been frighteningly inhuman. His discipline is of an order that is religious in its fanaticism, and his determination is such that soon he will start having ice-cold baths so that he can start the day fresh. Jumping into those baths filled with cubes of ice, he looks like a seal on holiday. The difference between him and the monks is that theirs is a life-long vocation. I wonder how Barry will react to normal life.

The Orange Parade is Protestant voodoo. More than anything, it is meant to keep the world view of popery at bay. The drums were banged long into the night to keep at bay a lifestyle that led millions of Irish people into the starving ditches. The message the drums beat out is hard work, thrift and independence, qualities that the man in room number seven has in abundance. Maybe that's why the Protestant people of Ulster have taken him to their hearts.

SUNDAY
19th May

Sunday is a day of rest. Sandra has come to visit Barry and Blain has come to see his daddy. As McGuigan trains in the old Rocky Marciano style, Sandra stays with Blain at the other side of the house. The contact is of the daytime variety. It suddenly strikes me that while I have been admiring Barry's dedication and discipline, I have forgotten Sandra's. For the next few weekends she will drive to Bangor from Clones, talk to Barry for the whole day and then go off to her own little bedroom with Blain. When in Clones she has to keep the house going and work in the hairdressing salon.

On Sunday night Gerald Hayes arrives. He is to coach Barry for the next few weeks. He has been over once before as a sparring partner, but now he is semi-retired from the game, which means that he will fight only if the money is right. Gerald has fought six world champions, including Pedroza. He has fought the best in the business, Chacon, Arguello, Lockridge, Pintor and Laporte. Gerald Hayes was what they call 'the opposition' in boxing. Too dangerous ever to get a title shot, he was willing to go anywhere. His story of his fight with Pedroza is astonishing. They fought one weight up from feather in the super-featherweight division. Pedroza looks well overweight in the fight clips. 'It was a quick weigh-in,' says Gerald with the tired knowledge of an old pro. He flew to Las Vegas, only to be told that the fight had been rerouted to Panama. So, like a true professional, he flew on to Panama. He was twenty-four hours non-stop in transit before he stepped into the ring. Then, astonishingly, he caught Pedroza with a right in the third round and landed him on his seat. In the tenth Pedroza hit him with a few but, as Gerald says, he never took a step back. The referee intervened to award a technical KO to Pedroza. The Panamanian was ahead on points at the time but they were taking no chances before a home crowd.

Gerald is a non-stop talker. He has seen videos of the Laporte fight with McGuigan and he says Barry was doing a lot wrong. In America, where managers know how to name themselves, Johnny Boss recommended Gerald as the best to Eastwood. Gerald Hayes didn't make much money from the fight game. He had two things going against him: one, he was just another black fighter in a division where the purses are normally small, and two, he didn't have a manager like Eastwood.

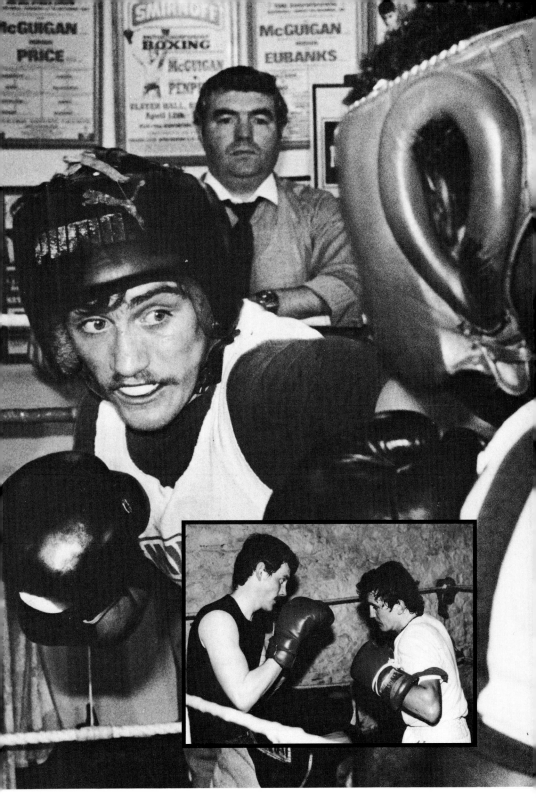

18 *(above)*. Trainer Eddie Shaw keeps a watchful eye on what's happening *(Pacemaker Press International)*

19 *(above, inset)*. Barry and brother Dermot facing up to each other *(Duncan Raban)*

20 *(top)*. Eastwood lays down the law to Ramos Yordan, the W.B.A. supervisor. Stephen Eastwood is in the background, Paddy Byrne to the right *(Pacemaker Press International)*

21 *(above)*. The scene at Loftus Road, Saturday, 8 June 1985 *(Pacemaker Press International)*

22 *(right)*. Everyone is backing Barry at the Pedroza fight *(Star)*

23 *(above)*. The knock-down in the seventh round which turned the title fight McGuigan's way *(Pacemaker Press International)*

24 *(left)*. Christodoulous shows obvious concern for a great champion in the thirteenth round *(Star)*

25 *(right, above)*. The nobility of the champion as he concedes defeat *(Star)*

26 *(right, below)*. Celebrating victory with Barney Eastwood *(Pacemaker Press International)*

27 *(left)*. The morning after the night before – Barry and family at the Holiday Inn *(Star)*

28 *(right)* and 29 *(below)*. Coming back in triumph to the biggest crowd in Belfast since V.E. Day *(Pacemaker Press International,* right, and *Star)*

30. Clones prepares to greet its most famous son *(Star)*

From today Barry starts to keep a diary ... what he eats
and how much he spars. There's not much else to record.
There is precious little else he does except conserve energy.
The first entry of note he makes is 'Please God the interviews will end tomorrow'. Gerald Hayes is almost the
extreme opposite to Barry as a personality. He is highly
voluble and is not afraid of expressing his opinions to all
and sundry. For the past eight days Barry has been getting
constant attention from the press. The only time they can
get to talk to him in peace is when he is eating, so interviews
are conducted over breakfast, dinner and lunch. The most
wearying part of the interviews is the constant repetition
of detail. That's what a public figure expects and Barry
handles the media perfectly. He has the ability to be himself
most of the time. Given the fact that the peace issue has
assumed such an important dimension, especially for the
American press, he has to be constantly on his guard as to
what he says. Asked his political opinions, Barry asks the
interviewer, 'Do you want this interview to end here and
now?' Irish history is so complex, it's like being asked to
walk across Niagara Falls on stepping stones. Some of the
stones appear solid, well-embedded and have names like
Peace, Charity, Hope and Love, but anybody who has tried
to cross will tell you that the rocks are as slippery as eels.

Over dinner he is asked how the death of Young Ali
affected him. He tries to give as precise an answer as
possible without becoming oversentimental, and at the
same time not to dismiss the most traumatic event of his
life with a shrug. It's not good psychologically for him to
be thinking about death in the ring so close to the most
important fight of his life, but there is the danger that
constant repetition of the same story will leave a dangerous
gap between his real emotions and the ones he must constantly repeat for the newsreel.

Today Barry parks his shōgun in the car park in Chapel Lane and goes across the road into St Mary's Church. He blesses himself as he goes through the door and turns to the statue of St Anthony. He holds the left foot of the saint and says his own private prayer. Then he picks up his bags and heads for the gym. This is the last day for the press, and again the gym is crowded. The television lights have turned the gym into a hot-house. Gerald Hayes stands at the side of the ring and keeps up a Joycean stream of consciousness throughout the sparring. 'Feint and throw the right. Feint and throw the right. Keep the right foot back. Walk him off the ropes, walk him off the ropes. Keep low. He's taller than you, his jab is going to be in your face if you don't keep low. You're too square-on. Turn your body, don't present such a big target. Keep your left shoulder up, chin well down in it. Get the weight on your right-hand side.' The press love the voluble Gerald. Ezekiel gets into the ring and the television lights go on full blast. The electronic bell rings and Barry and Ezekiel touch gloves in a friendly gesture. Ezekiel is moving with his usual cool confidence when suddenly, with his back to the camera, Barry catches him with a left hook. He takes four or five quick steps away and ends up dazed on the ropes. Barry slows down and asks, 'Are you OK?' It is the first indication I have had of Barry's extraordinary power. Ezekiel is twenty-one pounds heavier than McGuigan, but to watch them in the ring is to imagine you are watching two men of equal strength – until the cameras are turned on and McGuigan goes to work. It is the only glimmer we have seen in a week of McGuigan's punching power.

David Irvine and Peppy Muir start sparring. These are what's called the bottom end of the bill. Down there the punishment's just the same, sometimes worse. Last year Peppy broke his jaw and is only now recovering. Dave looks like a boxer fashioned in the public imagination. He has an attractive quality, but his face is well marked ... his nose flattened. 'I used to work for a car salesman,' says Dave as he skips. 'It was a job. There wasn't much else going. I had

to give it up. He didn't like me coming in with dark glasses.'
Dark glasses is boxing for the way boxers try to camouflage
their injuries. 'He didn't like the black eyes. It wasn't good
for his image. Now I just do a little bit of work for Mr
Eastwood and box.' Dave is on the London bill, trying to
avenge a defeat at the hands of the Scot, Dave Haggerty.
Eddie Shaw pays the same attention to the lads in the ring
as he did to the star of the gym. Peppy's arms and shoulders
are covered with tattooed characters and at the end of the
spar all of them are sweating profusely.

THURSDAY
23rd May

With the TV cameras departed, Monday slips into Tuesday, and Tuesday slips into Wednesday, which turns into
an undistinguished Thursday. The only common denominator for these days is hard work. In Barry's diary he will
record every day that he is getting caught too often and that
he is taking some really bad shots. He is desperately trying
to adapt to what Gerald Hayes is saying. By Thursday he
is confused. On the seafront he tries to work out what
is wrong. He knows that what Gerald Hayes is saying is
correct, only it seems to be for a different fighter. He is
desperately afraid of changing his style so close to the big
fight. 'What he is trying to tell me is OK for him,' Barry
says. 'Those blacks are more fluid than us. They move
easier. It must be the temperature they live in.' Barry has
his own unique style, with his centre of gravity low down,
working from a crouching position. Most of the time the
weight is on his left foot to accommodate his famous left
hook. Gerald wants him to switch to his right-hand side,
but McGuigan is terrified of losing the strongest weapon
in his arsenal.

About the only mental diversion Barry will have these days is the decision as to what number plate he should get for his new Lotus sports car. This is the closest he gets to a projection of ego. There are three or four choices, and the numbers begin to assume importance far above what they would in normal situations. They are like worry beads for Barry over the next few days. Significantly, he chooses 'BAX 1T' because that's the way they pronounce it in Belfast. 'BAX IT,' says Barry in his best Sandy Row accent. It's as if he needs something close to home.

With the clothes pulled up to his chin in bed, Barry suddenly looks like the teenager that won the Commonwealth championship in Edmonton. There is the look of the waif about him, lost, abandoned. He could have stepped out of the film *Oliver*. But this fragile-looking character has decided for himself that he must do at least ten rounds of sparring on Saturday to see how his fitness is shaping up. He's a glutton for punishment.

Late that night Eastwood and Gerald Hayes are discussing tactics up on The Hill. Eastwood is beginning to worry about Barry's training form. He is beginning to seriously worry, as they say in Belfast. We are watching a poor-quality video of Hayes versus Pedroza. At the start of the third round Hayes catches Pedroza with a right and the champion hits the deck. 'He's a sucker for a feint with the left and then a right cross,' says Gerald. Eastwood is listening intently. He knows that Gerald is a brilliant technician, but he is also aware that he is beginning to undermine Barry's confidence. Physically McGuigan is perfect, it's the tactical approach that is worrying Eastwood.

We watch a video of McGuigan versus Charm Chiteule, probably the hardest fight Barry ever had. 'They say McGuigan left it all behind him in the gym before this fight, but I don't know. Chiteule was a good boxer, maybe Barry just couldn't get to him.' For Eastwood even to intimate a negative comment about McGuigan, things must be at a low ebb. As we watch the video, Gerald is constantly enunciating what must be done in a nightmare litany. 'Feint with the left. Right foot back. He is setting up the shots but he's not throwing them,' says Gerald.

The amazing thing about Eastwood is that you can't see him thinking. Most people would show the wear and tear of the situation. There is the feeling with Eastwood that he listens to everything and then does what is necessary. Not what's right or wrong but what's necessary. He gets a phone-call from the manager of the Harris brothers. They have an appointment somewhere in the Welsh valleys, making it difficult for them to get to the airport. Eastwood wants them here on Friday. He needs familiar faces to counteract the Panamanians and Hayes. 'I will send a plane to pick them up,' says Eastwood. 'The plane will be there at ten in the morning; have your boys ready to go.' Eastwood's own private plane will leave Newtownards Airport next morning at eight o'clock. Before it does, Eastwood will make two phone-calls. First, he calls Joe Colgan, Barry's masseur from the amateur days, and then he calls the manager of Dwight Pratchett, the new North American lightweight champion. He too is packing his bags. One side of his luggage tag says Dwight Pratchett, Gary, Indiana, the other c/o Beresford House, Queens Parade, Bangor, Co. Down.

FRIDAY
24th May

By Friday night the Harris brothers have arrived. They quickly strike up a friendship with the Panamanians and Gerald Hayes. That night there is a disco in Bangor and all the boys go off together in the best of form.

While they are away McGuigan is in the little room that connects the dining room to the kitchen. He is pouring water into a pair of gloves. 'Loosen them up,' he says to the question that doesn't need to be asked. McGuigan uses every opportunity to focus his concentration. What for others would be a chore he turns into a ritual to loosen some valve that will allow his mental approach to be fine-tuned. It is not simply that a little water will make the gloves more flexible, more importantly it allows McGuigan to get to know them. He applies the same meticulous approach to every item of clothing and protective gear. By the time he steps through the ropes, even in a spar, he likes to feel that he has reduced the variants in the situation to a position where he can control them. Then he lets everything go. Which is why it is ultra-important that he can trust Eastwood and those in his corner. They become extensions of his own internal dialogue. When you are talking to McGuigan about the fight it's not a question of opinions and response. What he needs to feel is that whoever he is talking to is on his wavelength and that his own thoughts are finding vindication in the outside world. His will-power is so strong that he will just phase out negative opinion, however well intentioned. That strength can only come from some deep inner resource where he feels utterly secure. The word most often used by Eastwood about Barry is 'love'. It's not a word you normally hear in boxing.

To get through to him, one has to proceed on instinct and not try to rationalize his strengths and weaknesses into a shopping list. What he does is not rational. Boxing is not a rational sport ... cricket and soccer are rational sports. They are sports in which the violent side has been civilized and on the surface they appear a gentleman's game, but they frazzle with untapped violent energy. They are games for sophisticates. Boxing is raw and uncivilized with all its violent energy on display, and so it is the most international of all sports. They say that in some ancient societies the strongest men of the tribes fought to see which tribe would carry off the victory. In that situation the warriors fought for everybody in the tribe and their future. It still carries memories of that elemental social battle. In no sport are there more gangsters ringside and more saints in the ring. A boxing match seems to bring out the most violent side of human nature. I hesitate to say the worst of human nature because it seems self-evident that human nature is violent. Sometimes boxing, having brought out these ancient emotions, purges them. Rarely at a fight is there crowd trouble. Not to the same extent that there is at other sports.

McGuigan leads with will-power. He is not the kind of boxer who can be broken down like a machine into assemblable parts: a good right hook, strong chin, etc. The fighter Gerald is trying to fine-tune is an ideal fighter who presents the smallest target in the world and waits tactically until the opponent is open. There is a faint suspicion that that fighter might be of a dark complexion with the kind of supple body movements that make the limbo dance a national pastime. All of what he is telling McGuigan is correct, but it can only be grafted on to a very different style gradually. McGuigan's greatest asset outside of his will-power is his strength. His method is to get to his opponent and wear him down with superior strength. Pedroza is a master technician and will exploit all Barry's forward movement mercilessly. What seems to be difficult for Barry this week is to break down Jose and Ezekiel's style to individual parts and then exploit this in sparring. He seems to be taking the whole of their similar styles as given, and taking some punishment to learn about it. Barry's world view is consistent, open and whole; Gerald's is cagey, airy and experienced. There is a clash of world views going on here.

Today is the day Barry is going to do as many rounds as he is allowed. His diary reads: 'Got up 11.45, All-Bran, cup of coffee, one glass of orange juice. Gym 2 o'clock. 11 rounds spar.' At the end of two rounds' sparring with Barry, Peter Harris's nose is as black as a pint of Guinness. Peter looks upon it with the kind of friendly contempt one reserves for relatives who visit too often. With a shrug he passes off its appearance. You feel that he has had more condolences about it than a double widower. After three rounds with Ezekiel, Barry fights two with Jose. It's difficult to remember that all his sparring partners get into the ring fresh after he has gone through maybe three or more rounds. It's difficult because McGuigan never shows any signs of wear and tear. He always looks as fresh as his opponent. Now after ten rounds he is in the ring with Roy Webb, a boxer who is a division lighter than Barry. Roy won a silver medal at the Commonwealth Games, and as an amateur he was Irish champion. He is a good boxer, but he doesn't seem to be moving any quicker than Barry, and this after McGuigan has gone ten rounds with four different opponents. Barry has proved what we already knew: he is a superbly fit athlete with unlimited stamina. Apart from that, he has not fought spectacularly well for his high standard.

Today Jose and Ezekiel spar Peppy Muir and Dave Irvine. There is a big gap in class and experience. Jose is really performing. When McGuigan spars you never get the feeling that the other fellow is out of his depth. It's not that Barry comes down to their level, it's simply that he brings his performances up only a fraction beyond theirs. There is very little for the hare to learn in a race with the tortoise if he runs off miles ahead. There is also a feeling that McGuigan is aware of the potential humiliation involved. When others box there is a feeling of triumphalism when they are on top. With them it becomes a glorifying performance. Never with McGuigan; with him, it's almost an exorcism, some dark monster he has to overcome. Self-aggrandizement would amount to blasphemy. There are days when dark thoughts cross his mind. He has been caught by an elbow during sparring. 'This is the toughest game in the world,' he tells me. 'Some days after a really hard spar my memory goes for a moment. Like I'll be talking to you and suddenly I'll forget what I'm saying completely. It just goes out of my mind.' McGuigan pauses for a moment. 'What did I just say?' he adds with a smile.

WEDNESDAY
29th May

The Cliftonville Road runs off the Antrim Road on the outskirts of Belfast city centre. It is a mixed area which means it is neither wholly Catholic nor Protestant. It is a dangerous place to be when sectarian murder raises its ugly head. Dangerous for either denomination. The crime then is to be alive. For a time it was known as murder mile, and when they say that in Belfast they mean it. It's not the kind of place you'd pick up a lift late at night from passing strangers. About halfway up the road on the left-hand side there is a residence sheltered from the outside world by a high wall. In contrast to most other communities in Northern Ireland, it is not protected by barbed wire. This is the home of the Poor Clares.

When McGuigan looks for psychological succour he goes to a community whose lifestyle is more reclusive (and possibly more demanding) than his own. The Poor Clares live an austere life, as can be gathered from their name, but they do not cut themselves off completely from the outside world. They are painfully aware of it. Of all the people in Belfast, the Poor Clares are the closest mentally to the psychological consequences of the troubles. They try to mend invisible scar-tissue. Sister Pasquele will tell you that those who have suffered bereavement are amazingly charitable in their response. Loss seems to appease the lust for revenge. Their thoughts are constantly for the other poor mothers, fathers, brothers and sisters who will have to go through what they have already suffered. The Poor Clares are the unpaid psychologists of Belfast troubles. To them McGuigan is not an answer to the problems, or even the beginnings of a solution; but talking to him has helped to relieve some of the profound sadness they bear as witnesses to such suffering. Yet they know that hope begins with the smallest turn of the wheel. They will talk to Sandra, Barry's wife, too. They know that pain is non-denominational.

On Wednesday, 29 May, Sister Pasquele is waiting for Barry. He parks his shogun outside the gates and goes past the Sisters' private chapel into their house. In one room Barry gets a key which will open the door into another. A hand draws back the green curtain. Sister Pasquele and Barry exchange greetings. Barry can be certain that for the first time in weeks it won't be a heavy in-depth talk about boxing. He will leave with a simple assurance that the community will pray for him. Barry believes that prayer that issues from such deep knowledge and such silence is powerful. The visit will do him a world of good. Barry is the community's favourite visitor. That night at dinner in the refectory Sister Pasquele will casually mention that Barry was in to visit. No need for second names. Thirteen nuns will crowd around to see how he is doing and to hear how training is going, how Sandra is doing and what Blain is saying. Penance prayers and obligations will fly out the window for a moment. Sister Pasquele has one further ace up her sleeve. Normally the Sisters can only watch religious programmes on television but she has obtained a special dispensation for the community to watch the world title fight. The sight of thirteen nuns cheering McGuigan on has convinced me that Pedroza has no chance.

On Wednesday, 29 May, one of the reconnaissance helicopters from the Palace Barracks sent back a message that a large platform was in the process of construction just a mile down the road in the shelter of a bungalow. The bungalow itself was being renovated, but that might just be a cover for paramilitary activities. The barracks was well within the range of the IRA's rocket-launchers. The pilot of the helicopter radioed back that the work was being supervised by a middle-aged white-haired man. They worked long past twilight and the last cars' headlamps left the driveway just before midnight. Whatever work they were up to it was of an urgent nature. First dawn would see the reconnaissance helicopter leave the headquarters of the First Border Regiment.

When they flew over the residence that the computer called 'Broome Cottage' the white-haired man was already there, issuing orders. The instruments on this sophisticated flying bird told them that the platform was about twenty feet square. (They were two feet out.) A young soldier watched. Within minutes they would radio back to base that the mystery platform was in fact a boxing ring. Home base confirmed the computer's accuracy with one word: 'McGuigan'. The Eastwood on the computer was McGuigan's manager. One mystery was solved.

All day long the sun shone on the bleached white hair of Ned McCormack. He gave his last instructions in the early afternoon and prayed that the weather wouldn't change. Eastwood himself came down to congratulate Ned on the work. Then Ned was dismayed to hear Eastwood say that they wouldn't use it until late that night. Pressed for his reasons, all Eastwood would say was that it was 'psychological'. He wanted McGuigan to be getting into the ring at about the same time as he would in London.

The only people outside the camp who knew about it were those in the intelligence room at Palace Barracks – and they were likely to keep it a secret. They returned at three and then at four because they knew that the McGuigan party drove to the gym every day at about half-past two. They missed out. McGuigan didn't turn up for training until half-past seven. The only people there were those close to the camp: Trevor McClintock, Joy Williams and George Ace, along with the training team. Today Eastwood left Jose and his distractions in Bangor. Dwight Pratchett had proved to be an ideal sparring partner for Barry, and into the bargain he was a quiet easy-going mid-Westerner.

The ring looks huge in the back garden at Broome Cottage. It's a big ring, twenty-two by twenty-two. On a diagonal, it takes eight to nine paces to cross, but there is nowhere to run if you are in trouble. This is the size of the ring they will use in London. Eastwood is hovering around all the time talking to Barry. It's too late now to change much physically. Now all he can do is build on the patterns that have been developed over four years and refined a little in the past two weeks.

Barry boxes like the sun, brightly, brilliantly, without a stop. It's as if he has left all his problems behind in the gym. Eastwood is like a two-year-old, beaming like a child who has been promised candy-floss. Behind the childlike appearance however, the old yogi is thinking. He stops at seven rounds, almost annoyed that McGuigan wants to go on. They have reached some sort of psychological plateau, it can be only downhill from here. Amazingly, Eastwood won't allow McGuigan to train outdoors any more. It's as if he wants to preserve the memory of the outdoor boxing at Broome Cottage as some sort of little epiphany ... a small oasis on the Stations of the Cross. A blue sky, white ring and the best sparring so far is what will remain in McGuigan's mind. But after the fresh air it's back to the prison of room seven.

FRIDAY
31st May

The most important thing about Joe Colgan (apart from the fact that he is an excellent masseur) is that he knows Barry from the amateur days. With anybody else, some of Barry's energy would have to be displaced in formal introductions and the process of getting to know each other. Although Joe is one of the most prolific talkers in the game, this will not faze Barry. He can listen to Joe and faze him out whenever he wants, without any hurt taken or given on either side. Sometimes Joe will ask you a question and then answer it himself. Joe uses language like a message. You do not have to interpret everything he says or answer him.

I have noticed in the last few weeks that language is not as important to the boxers as the physical signals they receive. Their trade pre-dates language in the tribe. A week ago a video arrived from Teddy Atlas in the US. In it he was giving some instructions to Barry on how to fight Pedroza. Something was wrong with either the equipment or the cassette, because it was very difficult to hear the soundtrack. I was trying desperately first to correct it, and then, when it was fifty per cent right, to make out what was being said. After a few minutes I looked at McGuigan. He knew exactly what was going on. He didn't need to hear the words; he was watching a universal language.

Ireland is a country where language has run riot. At one time it was the only thing we could spend freely, and so it was dispensed with all the liberated wealth of the slave turned master. A lot of us Irish are caught in thought-patterns that are language- and not action-based. Emmet's speech from the dock is seen as a victory rather than the last hurrah of an ill-planned uprising. We are trapped by the faculty of speech, but the horror is that as Irishmen we can't communicate the bare essentials of humanity to each other. Like myself with the video, too many people listen and do not see.

FRIDAY NIGHT

After his big evening meal and his usual walk, it's time for Barry's battered body to get some relief. He lies face down on the improvised massage table just off the kitchen. Joe applies some oil.

'The only place I can see Barry improving is in the ring,' says Joe. 'For his height, his size, his whole body is in proportion. It can't get any better. You'll see guys with a great pair of shoulders and a little pea head. Barry's not like that, he's not freaky. He's got a great structure. He's a little Adonis.' Joe begins on Barry's back. 'Over the years Barry's got to know a lot about his body, the different muscles. He has developed each part of his body to perfection. He's got great stomach muscles. Great back muscles. Look, if you poured water on there it would just flow off. It's the muscles in the arms and shoulders for punch power. They are all connected like a girl's plaits. Twisted round and round and interconnected. The punch gains power not just from the biceps but from the muscles here in the chest and round the back, the pectorals and the deltoids.'

Barry by now is falling asleep. He has heard Joe's description hundreds of times and he is aware that Joe thinks Barry is the best amateur Ireland ever had.

'It's in the arms and shoulders for giving and in the legs and neck for taking. The legs are most important to any boxer. It's his foundation. You'll see boxers in the ring, they might have a powerful upper body but they get hit with a good shot and you'll see the legs going like what?' Joe answers his own question with one word, 'Jelly.' For a guy receiving a punch the most important thing is a good neck and strong legs. 'Am I right, Barry?' Joe asks, not expecting an answer. Barry growls in the affirmative. 'Am I right or wrong,' Joe asks as part of a tennis match he and Barry have played before.

'Exactly,' Barry drawls in almost as many tired syllables as there are letters. Barry moves on the table and starts to explain. 'The worst thing,' he says, 'is the jarring sensation. The more powerful your neck is, the more you can take it.' What's jarring is the brain. It's sitting there nicely protected by its own little crate, the cranium, when suddenly it is jarred by a blow out of nowhere. Barry has taught his body to react instantly to such an eventuality. He will ride with the punch. This has the effect of stopping the brain rebounding forcibly off the wall of the skull. The brain has its own particular suspension which can only withstand so much pressure before it passes on the impact. At that stage some of the motorized functions of the brain are impaired and, because of their position and length, the impact is most obvious in the legs. When the springs and supports that assist the brain are battered too much then they lose their elasticity and it's not long before the motorized functions spread their damage to every part of the body. Then it's not the legs that wobble but the speech.

Every day Dave McAuley kisses his wife Wendy goodbye and heads from his home in Larne towards Belfast. Today he will pack all the clothes he needs to keep him in London for a week, along with his training gear. Dave is slightly smaller than Barry, fighting in the flyweight division. He is the next-best prospect in the gym. He appears relatively unmarked from his boxing career, which prompts the thought that the most ruthless boxers are those who don't look like boxers. If Dave wins his fight on the London bill, he will get a shot at the British title – which would mean that he wouldn't need to be on the same bill as McGuigan to fill the Ulster Hall; he would be a draw in his own right. The contest means a lot to him. That is one of the reasons he will not overextend himself in training today. It's too near the fight for heroics. Besides, being in the same boxing stable, as they so ignominiously call it, Dave and Barry are good friends, on the look-out for each other's welfare. It's in such conditions that Barry receives the worst injury of his sparring. Reaching out a long lazy left jab he pulls a muscle somewhere near his left elbow. Eastwood looks round the room. There are only five or six people about. All of them are sworn to secrecy. Time will tell how bad the injury is, but the psychological damage could be devastating if it plays on McGuigan's mind.

Time to leave Beresford House. Outside, Eastwood pulls up in his Rolls-Royce. Everybody else has left for the airport; McGuigan is on his own. For the last time he goes back into room seven to say a silent prayer and to pull into his physical being the psychic energy he has displaced all over the walls and ceiling of this hidden little room. His fears, dreams and hopes hang in the air. He gathers as much of the energy as possible and heads out to Eastwood in the car.

The atmosphere on the plane is jovial, just like any group going on a high adventure anywhere in the world, the only difference being that there are very few drinks sold. The man who sits across the aisle from me I have seen in the gym, but I am not particularly sure of his position on the team. He carries a long canvas container, the kind that would hold a fishing rod, except it is much too broad. It's about the length of a shotgun, but I can't see any need for such an instrument on our trip. Eventually curiosity overcomes me. 'That's the peace flag,' says a small dapper man who looks as if he might be a civil servant in a neatly tailored suit. He carries the flag solidly between his legs. 'I will carry it into the ring.' Billy remembers the time he carried another flag. 'I remember the day I went to Dublin. I was to meet Harry Taylor on the station at Victoria Street in Belfast. He didn't turn up. It was for the European championships. It was a Sunday, I remember, 1946 or thereabouts. It is probably the greatest memory of my life getting off the train at Amiens Street in Dublin. There was Father McGloughlin in his clerical uniform and President Carroll. When he saw me, Father McGloughlin threw his cap into the air and came running down the platform, and lifted me off the ground, just because an Ulsterman was there to represent Ireland at the European Games.'

It's part of the cancer of partition in Ireland to classify

people according to their religion when they are from Ulster. There is no sense of triumphalism about any of this man's stories, so my lazy classification of him as a Catholic is now in doubt.

'Then when I was asked to box for Ireland at the Olympic Games, T. D. Morrison, head of Northern boxing, called me into his office. I had carried the flag at the European Games and he asked me, if I had to fight for Ireland, at least not to carry the Tricolour round Wembley. In my absolute innocence I said to him I didn't know if I would have the honour. I was as proud to carry that flag for Ireland as I am today carrying the peace flag for Barry.' He says he's a Shankill Road man, born and bred. That seems to be my answer: he is a Protestant. I ask him, is he? Without any belligerence he tells me religion has nothing to do with it. 'McGuigan has no relation to the troubles. People just can't help loving him. Especially the womenfolk of today. He's such a nice fellow, it's my delight in life to have helped him in whatever sense I might have done it.'

I ask him what he thinks of him as a boxer.

'I try to liken him to Sugar Ray Robinson. He can build himself up to the degree required and that degree is a winning degree. I think McGuigan will win inside the distance.' A sign tells us to put on our seat belts. 'Here we go, here we go, here we go.'

Barry and Eastwood sit together on the coach into London. From now until after the fight they will be inseparable. Dermot, Barry's brother, is on the bus as well. We drive towards the Holiday Inn. Our route takes us past the Grosvenor House Hotel in Park Lane. This is where Young Ali met his death in the ring with Barry. I wonder what he must be thinking as we drive past. In the past three months this tragic event has appeared on the perimeter of my attention six or seven times. I wonder how many times in little ways it affects Barry. We head on down to Marble Arch and on to the Edgware Road. There are about twenty in the party and our luggage is blocking the little London side-streets. Outside the Holiday Inn there are four flags, the Union Jack, the Canadian flag, the Holiday Inn flag, and what must be the peace flag. It flies limply in the cool June air.

TUESDAY
4th June

Barry McGuigan wakes up on Tuesday after a fretful night to a throbbing pain in his left elbow. He needs treatment immediately. This is a multi-million-pound problem. When Eastwood hears the news, he has two reactions: the first is regret and the second is terror. What he is afraid of is that the news will leak and the papers will carry scare stories and McGuigan will be subjected to constant talk about his injury. He has to keep this injury quiet. Most people in this situation would pull down the blinds and pretend nothing has happened. Instead, Eastwood gradually lets the word slip through the camp over two or three days so that by Thursday there are nine or ten people going around keeping a secret that only they, Eastwood and Barry are aware of. Amazingly, it works. Nobody in the press suspects anything until after the fight. The odds stay the same, so even Eastwood's compatriots in the bookmaking fraternity live in blissful ignorance – and these guys can usually tell whether the eggs were scrambled or easy over. The whole episode tells me something about Eastwood and McGuigan. Neither of them ever complains.

Apart from the fact that it has a peace flag conveniently outside the door, another reason the Holiday Inn was chosen is that it is close to one of the biggest parks in London. Hyde Park runs away from Marble Arch for a couple of miles. The corner of the park that is nearest the hotel is Speakers' Corner. This is where you can speak sedition and get a clap for it. It works on the old British tradition that if you put a man on a soapbox, you render him harmless. Barry will go for a run in the park for the next few days. On his first day running he sees a party of four or five black men. It's Pedroza's team. Barry takes an alternative route. It's too early yet to meet. He's not going looking for Pedroza yet.

Back at the hotel, Barry is feeling tired after his run and there's a press conference at the Portman Hotel at noon. To steel himself, he has an ice-cold bath. He will train later. He is expected at the Thomas A'Becket gym in the afternoon. On the podium at the press conference there is a new face. It is that of Mickey Duff. And what a face ... it's the kind of face with a thousand stories to tell, depending on the occasion. Above a boxer's nose, eyes ever in flight survey the assembly as if to say, 'Who's out to get me today?' He waits for the moment when he can claim his part in the drama.

McGuigan as ever has the press at his fingertips. By now any statement that he makes of a positive nature almost has the stature of fact so that when he says simply, 'I will win,' everybody nods in the kind of unconscious agreement that was last seen at Stalin's fourth Party Congress. Eventually Barry, having kept the press happy and his elbow under wraps for half an hour, departs for the Holiday Inn. At the press conference *The New York Times'* journalist confesses that she has never covered boxing before, but that the editor wants a story on McGuigan, and while pardoning herself she asks Gerald Hayes to spell his name. This is Mickey Duff's chance. He begins with a big G, follows with a big E, then an R straight out of *Sesame Street*, and A from the start of the alphabet, an L that in his cockney accent feels like a warm place to be, and he closes his introduction with a D that is as pronounced as the D in 'how de'. Gerald Hayes mops his brow, as much as to say, 'Thank God somebody got me out of that, us blacks can't spell.' Hearing the laugh that emanates from the assembled reporters, Mickey Duff looks at the little piece of mime Hayes is engaged in and smiles a big broad grin that says, 'It's all show business, we're funny guys up here, me and Gerald.'

Somebody asks, will there be drink on sale; Stephen Eastwood hedges his bets. This is a delicate subject with the Eastwood camp. They hate the image of the drunken Irish. But Stephen is annoyed that the British Boxing Board of Control have announced there will be no drink on sale; in the first place it's not their business, and in the second place it issues those who do want to see the fight through rose-tinted glasses with a forewarning to turn up legless.

Somebody asks if it is the biggest fight ever in Europe. Mickey sees another chance: 'It's the biggest fight since Henry Cooper fought Cassius Clay at Wembley Arena in 1962.' As I am thinking that is the first time I have heard the name 'Cassius Clay' in public in years, somebody corrects Mickey from the floor. Mickey listens and then again begins in a regal tone: 'I apologize, my friends, it was at Wembley Arena in June 1965. I ought to remember, because it was the week my son was bar-mitzvahed.'

'But you forgot, Mickey, that the man's name at that time was Muhammad Ali.'

Mickey smiles up and down the podium at his gaffe, as much as to say, 'Sure they don't believe a word I say anyway.'

Back at the hotel, Eddie Shaw and Barry train in the quiet of the penthouse. Barry does two or three rounds' skipping ... two on the pads and two rounds shadow-boxing. All through the routine Barry feels tired. From now on he begins to dry out. More than anything else, it's the physical manifestation of the upcoming battle. With the thirst come the nerves, which make the thirst worse. Without the nerves things would not be natural. So for the time being Barry is feeling thirsty and nervous and normal. At the Thomas A'Becket gym the caretaker will tell the assembled press, 'McGuigan won't be here today but certainly tomorrow.'

Early Wednesday morning, Barry goes for his last run before the fight. Back at the hotel, Danny lets Barry in for breakfast. Danny has been Barry's minder since the early days. Danny is as big as his personality. I've noticed the bigger the man is, the more he admires Barry. Danny's admiration shines out of his eyes at all hours of the day and night. This job minding Barry is different from Danny's usual police activities, but his disciplined, quiet presence is exactly the kind of company Barry needs in these last few days. Danny is always apparently relaxed but as alert as an actor on first nights. If all the men in the vicinity were asked to give their left arm for McGuigan, there would be a lot of one-armed men in the penthouse.

Barry's elbow has responded to the treatment, and there is less swelling. At two-thirty, Barry starts to train again in the penthouse. He does about thirty minutes altogether between shadow-boxing, skipping and the pads. The reporters at the Thomas A'Becket are again disappointed. McGuigan is getting the reputation of Howard Hughes. He has spent ninety per cent of his time since arriving in the penthouse. All he has for company is Eastwood and Danny and occasional visitors. If the truth were known, it's worse than that: most of the time in the penthouse McGuigan spends in his own room. He makes occasional sorties to the fridge for ice to have a cold bath. Eastwood and Danny only talk to him after he addresses them. Tomorrow at last Barry must leave the room. According to the WBA regulations there has to be a trial weigh-in two days at least before the fight.

The weigh-in is to take place in the gym in which Pedroza works out. According to the arrangements, the two fighters are to be weighed in separately, the first meeting to take place at the official weigh-in on Saturday. This unofficial version is a medical precaution to prevent the fighters losing too much weight close to the contest. They have to weigh in within five per cent of 9 stone, which would make 9 stone 6 pounds safe enough.

The gym is in Carnaby Street. I go down a dark flight of stairs to a basement. In a brightly lit gym two men are sparring. One of them I don't know, but the other is the longest reigning champion in any division. This is the legendary Eusebio Pedroza who has had more defences than any man since the great Joe Louis. This is what McGuigan has been hearing about since he was seventeen. From the day he won the Commonwealth gold medal at Edmonton, the name of Pedroza has stood at the top of the world's featherweights, as immovable as the Ten Commandments. This is the word made flesh, *El Campeon Mundial de Peso Pluma*. The action in the ring is unreal after the level of aggression at McGuigan's workouts. The boxers glide round the ring, bent double like two grannies exchanging notes about crochet. They throw light punches at each other, then show one another the punch that could do the damage without landing. The immediate feeling with Pedroza is of a king at the end of a game protecting his territory with masterful, simple moves. McGuigan on the other hand is as exciting and unpredictable as a knight errant, but if this fight is to be dictated by a preconceived tactical pattern, then the champion looks a past master.

On the T-shirt of one of Pedroza's cornermen are the words PARTIDO REVOLUCIONIRA DE LOS TRABAJAD-DORES. What that means translated into English is that Pedroza is a legislator in the Panamanian assembly for the

Revolutionary Democratic Party. Only six of Pedroza's defences have been in Panama; it is not the richest country in the world, and Pedroza has had to go wherever the money was best. He will get more for the fight with McGuigan than for his first eight defences put together. For a poor boy whose family lived in the broken-down shacks that housed the canal workers, one of the only ways upwards was through fighting. In the last couple of decades there have been seventeen Panamanian world champions. Each one of them receives a stipend from the government of £400 a month as a token of appreciation. Pedroza's hero and mentor was the General, Omar Torrijos Herrera. He was the kind of man Graham Greene went to Panama to vilify and remained to praise. He negotiated a treaty with the US that gave Panama control of the Panama Canal. Four years later he died in a mysterious plane crash. For Pedroza, the politician trying to better the lot of his people, possession of the world title is almost as strategically important for him as control of the canal is for the people of Panama. In that country most things revolve around the canal. His two trainers, who glory in the names of Henry Douglas and Lyonel Hoyte, are descendants of Jamaican immigrants who came to build it. Pedroza knows the power of a man fighting for a whole nation. He can detect somewhere on the perimeter of his radar that McGuigan means as much to the Irish people as all the seventeen world champions rolled into one. He doesn't fully understand why, but he has heard of Belfast and he will not go there to fight . . . and Pedroza will go anywhere in the world.

The rest of Pedroza's workout is a revelation. He attacks the heavy bag with a maniacal fury, landing punches from all angles. He skips in front of the mirror, urging himself on in inspirational Spanish, all the time letting out strange war-whoops which are translatable in any language as 'Kill'. Another cry is translated by a sparring partner from New York City as 'McGuigan is bullshit'. Pedroza understands that word. He confirms with a look and then adds in derogatory English, 'Bullsheet.' All the time Pedroza is urged on by Hoyte and Douglas, whose combined age is somewhere around one hundred and fifty years. Their bodies are twisted into the shape of men who might have picked cotton for seventy years. It's not just a world title that McGuigan threatens to take away from these men, he threatens to take away their world. What they don't know about the fight game you couldn't sell for fifty cents in Caledonia, Panama City's Harlem, the place where they were born and bred.

One figure stands out from the rest in the Pedroza camp. He has a name as impressive as his pleated white shirt. Mr Santiago del Rio feels like a man who, having just signed the best contract of his life, fears that it might be his life contract, and that the terms are not really as impressive as he had first thought. The Mephistopheles who got him into this situation is Mr Barney Eastwood. He has bought out all the options so that their whole future depends on defending the title successfully, in front of a slightly partisan crowd of 25,000 halfway round the world and, yes, I suppose you could say that Santiago is on edge. It's the kind of edge that knows all the ropes. He knows every trick in the book. When McGuigan doesn't show up at the appointed hour, he starts telling the press that it is a calculated insult to them. Trying to turn the press against McGuigan is like King Canute trying to turn back the tide. Santiago himself hasn't the gift of tongues and each voice he hears is speaking an unidentifiable language. In these situations, persistence gains more in stature than communication, and one man is very persistent. To add to his stature he has the initials ILHGA on the pocket of his blazer. He has been promised an audience with the champion. Santiago del Rio is pointing to the watch and asking the man with the initials, 'Where is McGuigan?' A messenger arrives. 'Eastwood understood that Pedroza did not want to meet him so why is he an hour and a half behind his schedule?' Santiago listens to the translation and then says, 'OK, if they are afraid to meet us, we go ahead with our weigh-in, McGuigan can come in when the champion is finished.' He promises that Pedroza will stay in his dressing room until McGuigan is gone. Pedroza has now been at full tilt for over an hour . . . He must be having weight problems. He moves towards the scales. Santiago del Rio stands to his right. They weigh him. The crowd hear 8 stone and the rest is lost in a gasp. The champion is underweight already. This will have a psychological effect on McGuigan. Pedroza does not need to work hard any more to lose weight. He holds his index finger up in the air. '*Numero Uno*,' he says in international language.

The man from the I L H G A is talking to Pedroza. The press is waiting for McGuigan. Somebody from the Pedroza camp says McGuigan is scared. Pedroza moves away from the man with the initials. 'Where is he going?' asks somebody from the press. 'To the dressing room,' says the man with the initials. 'Where is McGuigan?' somebody asks. Nobody knows. 'Who is in charge?' asks a press man. Somebody asks the man from I L H G A what the initials stand for. 'Oh that,' says our man, 'that's the Irish Left Hand Golfers Association.' The mad hatter has taken control.

Another crowd moves from the door towards the weighing scales. The empty space in the middle is occupied by McGuigan. There is no more telling difference between their heights than the fact that McGuigan is not visible until he steps on to the scales. He strips close by and then the pale small frame ascends the scales. 8 stone 13 pounds and some ounces. There is an ounce or two in it. It's unbelievable that the two men weigh the same, given the difference in frame. McGuigan makes no gestures.

Pedroza's animal energy is different from that of McGuigan. Pedroza can summon huge reserves at will. With McGuigan it is ever present. It's as if that animal force uses Pedroza's body as a diving instrument through which it passes so that in the gym you will know where he is because of the waves he makes through the crowd. McGuigan simply does not displace that amount of energy.

Pedroza emerges from the dressing room. In the boxing

lexicon the word they use to describe him is dour. It's a word that short-changes the man. It's just that his smile is detached from his eyes. The bottom half of his face has learned to be a politician, but his eyes are those of the ghetto in the land of plenty. He watches McGuigan for a time.

Carefully Pedroza puts on a cap that would do a lumber-jack proud, the kind of cap they issue in the baseball little leagues in Panama ... the kind that adds three or four inches to your height. He adjusts it to get the maximum benefit. As McGuigan heads towards the exit, he comes forward and holds his hand out. McGuigan reciprocates the gesture. They shake hands. They freeze. Pedroza's face is smiling, but his eyes are not. McGuigan pulls his hand away and heads for the exit. Later, Pedroza will claim that McGuigan was scared. On the way out Barry meets Ove Ovesen, the Danish judge. 'Ah, Ove,' says Barry, 'I remember you from when you were refereeing the ...' If he has such presence of mind when he's scared, what's he like when he's fearless?

THURSDAY NIGHT

Besides the weigh-in there are other obligations on this Thursday. It is the feast of Corpus Christi and Barry goes to eight o'clock mass around the corner from the Holiday Inn. I try to remember which Station of the Cross we are sitting behind; it's only later that I realize it was Christ meeting His stricken mother. Barry is praying intently. At home, Sandra has journeyed from Clones to Belfast to speak with the Poor Clares before she goes on to London. She will stay at a guest house in Kilburn, well out of Barry's way, until the fight is over.

Back at the hotel, Eastwood is pacing up and down his

room. McGuigan is in the room beyond. Between the rooms are two doors. Eastwood's is open all the time. When McGuigan opens his, Eastwood knows he wants to talk. Until then, he keeps an almost silent vigil. The press have been looking for Barry all week, but they have been kept at bay. McGuigan has spent most of the time in his own room, opening the door occasionally to talk about old stories, small talk, nothing important.

Suddenly Eastwood stops. 'I was standing here,' he says, 'and he was standing there. I said to him, "This bigotry is terrible. If you come from the country it's not too bad though it's bad enough there, but if you come from the Shankill or Falls Road, it's bred into you." He looks at me with the eyes. "Something will have to be done about it, Mr Eastwood," he says. "What's your idea, Barry?" I says. He says, "All the grandparents and great-grandparents, shag the lot of them. If we started off now, all the young people. It's our country, let us all live in peace. No more of this ******** bigotry. Bring your children up and say, 'So you're a Protestant, you're a Catholic.' Live with them, mix with them. Marry them. Get involved with them and vice versa. You see; in ten years the improvement would be terrific." ' Eastwood pauses for a moment. 'In the House of Commons he would have got a standing ovation.' We tiptoe back into the room with the ice in it.

Eastwood tells me of the time he went to Haiti to see the Laporte–Gomez fight. Out of Gomez's corner came this voodoo woman. Everybody laughed, but Eastwood remembers the look in Laporte's eyes. 'When Pedroza gets into the ring, I'm going to produce this midget from under the ring. I'll have him stored there from early on, and then at the appropriate moment we'll produce him. I'm going to get him to go over to Pedroza and shake his fist. An Irish leprechaun. What'll he think?' Eastwood asks the question, knowing full well what he'll think.

Friday is one of those days that you can never anchor. The ship sails on over incalculable depths which nobody can sound.

At a meeting in the Imperial Hotel there are seven men. Six of them are men made flesh, the seventh is the ghost of Brussels. It's only a couple of weeks since the Liverpool–Juventus Cup Final at which nearly forty people died. 'How will the crowd react if a man is counted out after the bell at the end of the round,' asks the referee, Stanley Christodoulous. The importance of the crowd is stressed again and again. Santiago del Rio is not here, so Eastwood can relax. He leans forward and whispers. All the heads lean in and consider what he is saying. When they lean back they look as if they have been taken into the confidence of a man who will go as far as possible to accommodate anything they want.

Eastwood continues to confide in them: 'Santiago del Rio wanted American gloves, then he wanted English gloves, then he wanted gloves from anywhere in the world. I told him he could have American, English, South American, Italian, anything he wanted.' The grin with which Eastwood says it could mean any number of things. Now Eastwood is in his stride. 'Look at the tape situation. He wanted unlimited tape, then he wanted ten feet of tape, then he wanted something else. I told him we'd fight any way he liked, no tape at all if that's what he wanted.' Everybody laughs a little. Everybody knows that the rule says ten feet of tape, but the bravura with which Eastwood announces things endears him to everybody. Eastwood epitomizes the difference between the con man and the artist. With the artist you know you are being conned and you love it.

The public rules meeting will take place at the Portman Hotel. All over West London the lights are out. In the foyer of the hotel a lone harpist, undisturbed by the enveloping gloom, plays a melancholy air. As we begin our ascent up the dark stairs, the harpist resolves the cascading strings into the Beatles' 'Michelle'. We turn up a second flight, to be met by a generous window that allows the meeting to be held in some kind of twilight.

Santiago del Rio is there, as accommodating as a well-fed cat in the absence of Eastwood. Everything is resolved quickly.

Back at the Holiday Inn, Eastwood is exploding. 'I don't care what ABC says, that's not the way it's being done. I don't care about their money. They can take the money and go back to the States. I have the cheque downstairs. I haven't cashed it yet. I don't care about prime time or half time or any other kind of time, Pat McGuigan is singing "Danny Boy" and he's singing it for 1 minute 45 seconds. I got Phil Coulter to arrange it, 25,000 people will join in. When Pedroza hears it, it will send shivers up his spine. You can come up here to the penthouse now but I won't change my mind.'

Eastwood storms around his side of the penthouse. Over on the other side Father Salvian Maguire is saying mass for Barry. The grey-haired Father Maguire is a Passionist father who bears the marks of having listened to a hundred thousand confessions all over Ireland. Today he heard morning confessions then drove to Belfast to take the plane to London to say mass for Barry, as has been his custom ever since they became friends. Everybody has that look about them that says, 'Let's stay calm,' but the atmosphere is electric.

The phone rings again and Eastwood picks it up. 'Hello, Mickey,' he says. 'Sure the boy is calm. He can stand up to the pressure. I never saw him so calm. There's been an awful lot of money for Pedroza. There was one bet of 50,000 and another of 60,000 and several of 25,000. They rang Adrian at the head office and asked, could they lay some off. Adrian said he could lay 25,000 without thinking but if it was any more he'd have to call me. I told them they could have 100,000 and when I say 100,000, maybe they could have a bit more. Do you think maybe they are trying to check us out? Would they have heard about McGuigan's elbow, do you think? The only person I can think of with that sort of money in cash is Pedroza. Is he backing himself? Yes, check the odds in Las Vegas and ring me back.' Eastwood hangs up the phone. He asks the air, 'Who is backing Pedroza for that sort of money?'

Arrangements are made to get Father Maguire a room to stay in. McGuigan is in his room on his own, but his unseen presence haunts the sociable side of the penthouse, the way the ghost of Parnell haunted Irish politics for decades. McGuigan has used up all the ice on the eleventh and twelfth floors. We have to get Ross Mealiff, Sandra's brother, to go two floors below.

Eastwood starts to talk. He talks the way McGuigan boxes. In public he is reserved, quiet, aware that the talk is for general consumption, but in private his talk is like a succession of hammer blows. When he talks about the McGuigan–Pedroza fight, it's as if his words have some magic quality capable of influencing the event ahead. He looks into his glass as if he can divine the future in there. 'Look, here's what it's all about, boys. There's nobody knows as much about Pedroza as I do. There's certainly nobody on this side of the Atlantic. I could tell you the colour of his wife's eyes, I know so much about the man. He's a legendary fighter. He's the fighter for the connoisseur. He mightn't suit the Falls Road man or the Shankill Road man, who want to see two guys battering each other, but the cuteness of him, the way he can block and move! He can do it all. The wee short ones he can hit you with, and he can stamp on your toes. He's got the cunning, he's got the craft, he's great at all the naughty stuff but, look, I've said to Barry, he's an old man. He could be your dad. You've got the strength, you're twice as strong.' Eastwood pauses. 'He's real hungry to win.' Then he adds ominously, 'He's got to win for all of us.'

When Eastwood says all of us, he doesn't mean the people in the room or Barry's mother and father or the people at the fight or the Catholics and Protestants watching in their separate pubs and homes in Belfast, or the Irish throughout the world. He means everybody. It's as if mankind itself would benefit from McGuigan winning. That's the kind of way he believes in the Cyclone. This mystical faith in McGuigan is both frightening and compelling.

Eastwood continues: 'There's a wee signal that he's been saying to me all week without saying anything at all. He's saying, "I'm ready," without saying anything at all.' Eastwood pauses in imitation of McGuigan's silent communication. Their strength comes from silence. 'You see the eyes. It's the eyes. You see he'd be doing something there and we're just footering about and he'd look up like that ... Sssush,' Eastwood makes a noise that primitive man might have made to describe a charging bull. 'Just like bullets coming out of his eyes. You couldn't describe it.' He just has. He holds everybody spellbound, describing an energy most of us have not felt since our childhood. A passionate anger beyond logic. 'If I'm any judge of a fighter, this guy is going to produce everything tomorrow night.' With that the beginnings of 8 June start. We go to bed at dawn. The weigh-in is at ten o'clock.

SATURDAY MORNING
8th June

On Saturday morning, Barry is still in great form. Eastwood is up early, trying to protect this mood. The Friday night papers have been talking about Barry's sombre mood of resignation. He has been totally isolated at the top of the Holiday Inn for almost a week and he is gaining a reputation Howard Hughes would have envied.

At seven o'clock that morning, Pedroza has weighed in privately at the Leicester Square Odeon. Stephen Eastwood is there with Trevor McClintock. They are not allowed within twenty feet of the weighing scales. Pedroza steps up and Santiago del Rio adjusts the scales. He says, the entourage translate, 'Nine stone,' and they clap each other on the back.

With McGuigan there is no problem making the weight – although there *is* a problem making the scales, as there are more people at the weigh-in than were at his first half-dozen fights. Barry and Eastwood push their way towards the stage. It's ten o'clock and they should be weighing-in by now. Santiago del Rio, thorough professional that he is, points to his watch, saying in effect that McGuigan is late, his man is going to get up on the scales first. By this stage, Eastwood and Barry, with Danny and Vince McCormack protecting them, are halfway down the aisle. Pedroza steps on the scales and gets off quicker than the three-card-trick man. The scales nod for a moment and then come back to rest. Stephen Eastwood says he didn't see what happened, and then his attention is caught as he sees McGuigan climb on to the stage.

Things are about to die down when McGuigan says to Eastwood, 'Stephen is not happy, Mr Eastwood.' Eastwood catches McGuigan's words and fully understands his drift. He explodes. The dam of protection that he has been building round Barry has been burst.

With the same kind of hand–body movements that Michael Jackson and Mick Jagger use to whip a crowd into frenzy, Eastwood is all over the stage. Everybody is culpable. To look at it objectively you would say that he has gone over the top. His eyes have the same kind of maniacal fury that Ali had before his first fight with Sonny Liston. Everybody is astonished at the performance, but what nobody knows is that McGuigan caused it. One little word of doubt from him is enough to send Eastwood down to hell, to bring back the fire of self-belief. This is what McGuigan needs to retain that calm that has descended

191

like a gown of snow around self-doubt. He knows that Eastwood will let nothing pass.

For his part, Eastwood believes in his soul that, given a fifty-fifty chance, McGuigan can take the title. He is pointing to Pedroza and then pointing to the scales. You don't need a translator to know what Santiago del Rio is saying: 'He crazy – he loco.' They are staying where they are. Their trial is over. Nothing can calm Eastwood; he stalks about the place. He asks Ray Clarke of the British Boxing Board of Control, 'Is this the way we are going to be treated?' It looks like the fight is off now, because Eastwood won't let McGuigan go ahead until Pedroza is put on the scales again. Santiago del Rio sees his chance and Pedroza is out through the door.

Quietly McGuigan goes over to Eastwood and says, 'Let's go ahead.' Immediately Eastwood goes to the scales. Mickey Duff wants to make an announcement, but Eastwood grabs the microphone. 'The way we have been treated is a disgrace. I hope we are not treated as bad tonight. They have won all the rounds so far, we are going to start winning from the first bell tonight.'

The British press are aghast. No stiff upper lip here. Suddenly the weight of what McGuigan is fighting for has shown in Eastwood's reaction. From now to fight time, he will be as calm as McGuigan. The thunder has spoken.

SATURDAY EVENING

The rest of Saturday passes quickly. Barry spends the day eating, filling himself up with carbohydrates. Dermot is there most of the day. He and Barry exchange jokes. At seven o'clock the bags are packed. It's time to go.

'Make sure you have everything now,' Eastwood says.

'Can we get out of here quietly?' We press the lift button that only has one direction on the twelfth floor. It seems to take forever.

'Anything but boxing now, do you hear me, lads?' Barry says, and then adds, 'please.' Still the lift is not here. Barry again:

> 'One fine day in the middle of the night,
> Two blind men got up to fight,
> Back to back they faced each other ...'

No need to guess at Barry's dreams now. Somebody moves impatiently at the lift's tardiness.

Eastwood responds:

> 'For a man he is fool
> For when it's hot he wants it cool
> And when it's cool he wants it hot
> And always wanting what is not.'

Here are two of the bravest men I have ever met talking nonsense rhymes before perhaps the most important night of their lives. But the rhymes have that ability to hold reality together as if they answered some deep, simple need: the subconscious nightmare of McGuigan and the wish fulfilment of Eastwood.

Eventually the lift arrives. We get in ... seven of us. We have an uninterrupted ride to the fourth floor where the lift opens to reveal a couple of tourists. Their way is barred with the magic word, 'Security.' Down in the bowels of the hotel feet echo in the car park. Ray jumps into the van. He has driven the route to Loftus Road many times, but still his nerves are on edge.

On the way McGuigan is telling most of the jokes. They are the kind of jokes that would be best appreciated in Clones. Mostly they are about local characters and their mannerisms. It's as if Barry is trying to remember who he is and where his roots are, like the Beatles and their early, overexaggerated Liverpool accents. The one that could apply to Pedroza gets the biggest reaction: 'He's so thin the one eye would maybe do him.'

A car has been following us for some time and Danny asks who it is. It turns out to be the Harris brothers, as carefree as if they were going to a carnival. We pull round Shepherd's Bush, and the traffic gets thicker. People going to the fight start to recognize McGuigan. Their faces light up in instant pandemonium. 'Go Barry, get him!' they scream. They roll down the windows of taxis at the same time as they open the door, their co-ordination lost in the tumult of their well-wishing. We drive on past the overflowing pubs. At five minutes to eight we pull up at the players' entrance at Loftus Road and are quickly lost in the narrow tunnels that lead to the dressing rooms.

The scene in the dressing room is in marked contrast to the world of the Holiday Inn and the good-natured press conferences. This is where the blow lands. It's stunningly easy to tell which fighters are getting ready and which fighters are getting repaired. Roy Webb's eye looks like something out of *Star Wars*: it has grown to monstrous proportions and along its hard-boiled circumference there is a gash an inch long from which I recoil, expecting every second a human eye to emerge and survey the passing caravan that troops into McGuigan's dressing room. Webb has won – I dread to think what his opponent looks like in the other dressing room. Paddy Byrne berates the texture of Webb's skin for its lack of resistance. 'That Webb fellow, he cuts too bloody easy,' he says with a child's sense of bafflement. 'I know he bloody well won,' says Paddy, 'but he cuts too easy.' Paddy's anger is with the epidermis of mankind, its tissue-like softness under attack. This mild outburst out of the way for the rest of the evening, Paddy will be the coolest man in Loftus Road. This outburst just serves notice that his adrenalin is flowing. He's on his toes.

The room has been picked for its defensibility. Only one door gains admittance and with his back to it, as immovable as Samson, stands Danny. McGuigan sits on the bed, cut off from the outside world by a field force that keeps his eyes focused on the floor. Looking at his eyes, I expect him every minute to turn into the Incredible Hulk. It's impossible to tell that there are other fights going on at this moment. To make sure that reality hasn't gone amiss I go out into the stadium grounds. Far away I see the illuminated square. One figure is on the canvas. I look at the TV monitor in the dug-out. The little beetle on all fours turns into the familiar figure of Dave McAuley. It's the fifth round. The referee is beginning to count. He beats the count and I go back to the dressing rooms.

Back in the dressing room McGuigan is under attack. Santiago del Rio has just burst through the door demanding to see McGuigan's bandages. The man doing McGuigan's hands, George Francis, is the best in the business. He has managed many world champions and, as they say euphemistically in boxing circles, 'he can take care of himself'. Santiago del Rio pushes George aside and suddenly it looks like the tension is going to explode prematurely here in the dressing room. He wants McGuigan's hands re-done. Suddenly the room is full of officials, translators, peace-makers and peace-breakers. Santiago is pulling at McGuigan's hands. It is an obvious attempt to break McGuigan's composure, and that is the only reason Eastwood keeps his cool. 'Get this man out of here before any damage is done,' he keeps repeating. It is decided to re-do Barry's hands. Again Santiago is not happy: 'The bandage cannot go near the knuckle,' he is translated as saying. Again, Vesuvius rumbles and McGuigan's eyes cloud over with a mist that is either anger on the boil or the tears of frustration. Dermot appears at the door and the protection that was tribal turns animal. This is the leader of the pack protecting the cub. This is a blood-brother on the rampage. He stares at Santiago del Rio. All need for translation goes out of the door. This is no play-acting. Another false move and all hell will break loose. The hands are shown to the officials. The referee comes in through the door. 'Of course the hands are O K.' Santiago del Rio moves towards the door. A half-smile plays across his lips at a job well done. It's the last time he will smile tonight.

I walk out to the tunnel again where Wendy McAuley, Dave's wife, is crying her eyes out. I am about to console her when she turns her eyes away. The St John's Brigade are carrying a stretcher into the dressing-room area. I look in horror at the figure, and then to my utter relief I see that he is fair-haired. It's the Scottish opponent, Bobby McDermot. Wendy's tears turn to relief and then to joy; Dave has won.

In the dressing room they are taking off his gloves. He broke his left hand in the third round. He had to keep throwing out the left jab for several more rounds so that his opponent wouldn't know that he was as predictable as a one-armed bandit. Dave's face looks like a boiled lobster. No sculptor would ever stretch the skin so far on such a small frame. Congratulations pour in from all sides. His fellow professionals say nothing. They know that victory smiles bring pain. Eddie Shaw takes the glove off with his ruthless delicacy. His hand has been inside that glove, too. In the tenth round Dave knocked his man out.

Davey Irvine is getting ready to go out. He seems calm and relaxed, but once you put on those gloves you know there's going to be pain. Like a pregnant woman, no matter what happens, there's going to be pain. Back in Barry's dressing room, Dermot is whispering to him. The next hour flies past and suddenly everybody is saying it's time to go.

Somebody asks, 'Have you got the iron, Paddy?' You can't forget things out there. Paddy is a true professional and so he has made a list of all the things he needs. What he needs most is calm. He needs the presence of mind of an airline pilot who never reacts in a hurry, no matter what the situation. 'Cut men' in the fight game are rogue surgeons. They need the cool of a surgeon and the touch of a faith-healer. Razor blades and ice are the alpha and omega of their trade and they strike while the iron is cold. The fighter depends on them for his vision. With a swift application of the iron they can add a second dimension when a boxer is fighting from one eye. Tonight, Paddy Byrne is one of the 'I've seen it all before' school, but deep down he knows it's never the same twice.

'Let's go,' McGuigan says with all the cool of a commando. He's ready. In that moment a burden is lifted. It's too late to stop now. We are sucked down the long corridor by a tremendous noise. Desire made manifest in the shape of one long inexhaustible howl that would be a continuous scream except for the fact that it breaks like waves, each succeeding one crashing into the slipstream of its predecessor. What depth of passion created this roar?

The long corridor to the ring has a life of its own, opening and closing like a demented accordion. Ahead, the peace flag mast-head of this crazy caravan dances on the edge of a whirlpool that constantly threatens to pull us down. Eddie Shaw is a boxer, he fights his way through the crowd. There is no etiquette in hell. Tonight the roar is McGuigan's theme song and the score from *Rocky* plays a muted second fiddle, like a crazy violinist reading from the wrong stand. For 25,000 people at a football stadium in London, McGuigan is not the Great White Hope, he's the only hope.

The swell ends at the no-man's-land where the paying public meet the ringside commentators. Viewed from outer space, McGuigan is the centre of a sparkling necklace as a hundred photographers try to pull reality down to earth in a flash. Reality tonight is a dream come true. McGuigan is getting into the ring to fight for the world title. Ireland is good news for once, and 25,000 people erupt as He Who Never Steps Backwards comes through the ropes. He dances forward. 'Buy land,' said W. C. Fields, 'they don't make any more of it.' McGuigan dances across the ring, each hook and jab a down-payment on this piece of real estate. For fifteen rounds tonight this space is up for grabs. A boo stifled at birth warns us that the other bidder is on the way, and then the boo turns into the sustained applause worthy of this world champion.

Now all the forces are assembled and it's time for the

national anthems. The British national anthem doesn't sit easy on the shoulders of 25,000 Irishmen, but eventually everybody behaves with the decorum invented in the heart of that other great empire ... for a couple of minutes we are all in Rome. Suddenly from nowhere comes a sound as remote as the theme from *Rocky* was. It's impossible to make it out in the din. Pat McGuigan, microphone in hand, answers this musical quiz with the deadly ear of the born crooner.

> But come you back when Summer's in the meadow
> and when the Valley's hushed and white with snow

Now everybody knows what it is and Pedroza looks around in belligerent defiance as the whole crowd join the chorus:

> 'Tis I'll be there in sunshine or in sorrow
> Oh Danny Boy, oh Danny Boy, I love you so.

These are 'the men that God made mad, For all their wars are merry and all their songs are sad'. If Pedroza is pulled in by the deceptively beautiful air then he's lost a psychological round. 'Danny Boy' is a recruiting song for war. It's a brilliant ploy from the Eastwood camp, uniting the crowd in a lull before the storm.

Now each corner has one last trick to play from its psychological armoury. True to form and with a little nod to Carl Jung, Eastwood produces his from a subterranean level. Paddy Byrne lifts the skirts of the ring and the dwarf emerges. They wait till Pedroza turns away and then the little man jumps into the ring. The crowd shouts. Pedroza turns and the look in his eyes is astonishing. It's as if for a moment he allowed his subconscious to think that this was McGuigan. If only it were so ... Reality returns and the cheekiness of the gesture demands a smile which Pedroza gives with a cool mastery. The MC's announcement of 'My Lords, Ladies and Gentlemen' is drowned out, presumably by the gentlemen. It's time for the seconds to get out of the ring. Eastwood feels something tugging at his sleeve. McGuigan looks around. '£5,000, my man at even money,' says Lyonel Hoyte. Eastwood looks into his eyes. '£5,000, my man will take him out,' repeats Hoyte. Eastwood looks for the green which is nowhere in sight and so he pulls away. Money talks, bullshit walks. There are no more ploys to play.

The opening round is marked by a combination of speed and phenomenal concentration. Pedroza's concentration is remarkable, given the fact that he is fighting on foreign territory – but then he has already performed in front of the grass-skirted warriors of Papua New Guinea. He has an amazing mind. He goes on his bicycle, shooting out long left jabs and keeping well out of McGuigan's way. The first solid blows are landed in the neutral corner where Dermot McGuigan has parked himself. They came from Barry. Dermot claps. McGuigan pursues the champion for the whole three minutes, but Pedroza wins the round with the effectiveness of his counter-punching.

Round two is much the same as round one, with one small exception. McGuigan, instead of following Pedroza around the ring, starts to cut off his territory. It's like the snake and mongoose, but Pedroza is not hypnotized. He leans down in the middle of the round, staring into McGuigan's headlamps. Fighting inside, Pedroza can use his famed bolo punch which comes from below like an upwardly mobile piston. In this round he also lets loose a strong left hook, but the inescapable fact is that he is not overwhelmingly superior inside. McGuigan has neutralized the Panamanian's greatest asset.

From his commentary position Harry Carpenter is shouting, 'This can never go fifteen at this pace.' The third is the start of thirteen rounds that will make a liar of him. At the opening of the third round Pedroza fights brilliantly, whipping in a punch that is a combination of an uppercut and a bolo. Pedroza is such a craftsman he invents punches. This one lands under the heart. It should have slowed McGuigan down. It didn't. McGuigan keeps coming forward, and now he begins to slip Pedroza's jabs and counters with his own hooks to the body. The champion is acting as if these are having no effect on him. McGuigan's cheeks are rouged from Pedroza's left jab, but he never looks in trouble. This is not just a physical contest, this is going to be a battle of minds. That both men are in perfect physical condition is obvious from the first nine minutes. At the end of three rounds, nobody is ahead in either the psychological or the physical battle.

At the start of round four, Pedroza hesitates. The bell goes to call them to the centre of the ring and the champion turns back to get his gumshield. It is the first lull in the action. It lasts only five seconds but it's like a blemish on perfection. Is it a conscious ploy of Pedroza's or his unconscious asking for respite? Pedroza has trained himself to go fifteen rounds. He has trained to go three minutes a round – but not like this, this is inhuman. Not since the legendary Henry Armstrong has a fighter thrown as many punches per round as relentlessly as McGuigan. Each one of them is intended to take Pedroza's head off. He knows he is in with somebody desperate to win, fearless and strong. Pedroza is the master tactician looking for time to work out his strategy. He isn't getting any.

Immediately the round opens, McGuigan catches him with a hard right. Pedroza shoots back a left hook and right uppercut. Most people at the ring think they see Barry smile as if the punches had no effect on him. He was in fact grabbing his gumshield in his mouth. McGuigan has two reactions when he has been stung: he grabs his gumshield tighter and he wipes off the gloves on his trunks as if to obliterate all that's gone before.

After that it's as if he's moving the contest on to a higher, more demanding level. It's this ability constantly to bring his performance up to the required level that reminds people of Sugar Ray Robinson. During the fourth and fifth rounds he wipes off his gloves on his trunks several times. Pedroza has only one answer: he must stand his ground. Somehow he has to stop this Niagara pouring over him. In the middle of the fifth, he tries to move Barry back. They stand toe to toe, exchanging orthodox and unorthodox blows. The kid is brilliant inside. And strong. Too strong. Pedroza decides to get on his bike again. This time he has a slow puncture.

Boxers are so alert physically in the ring that they sense what will later be revealed only by slow motion. At the end of the fifth round McGuigan sensed that Pedroza was slowing: he moved against the ropes in McGuigan's corner, looking for a breather. McGuigan didn't give him an inch. He loaded up to land the big one. When he threw out his long left jab he felt a tear at the elbow. The psychological advantage had been countered by a physical problem. McGuigan told his corner that his arm was acting up. Eastwood said he could beat Pedroza with one arm. He didn't get a chance to throw that arm until the seventh round.

Towards the end of the sixth round, a strong right to the body catches Pedroza. His knees buckle momentarily. Pedroza is hit with a strong overhand right. He stumbles and then looks to the ground as if he missed his footing and slipped. This man never gives out hurt signals. This is the technique Ali used against George Foreman until the champion ran out of heart. McGuigan's heart is as big as Loftus Road.

There's no faking the reaction to the right McGuigan hits Pedroza with at the end of round seven. His legs give out from under him and, before he can bring up his instinctive right arm in defence, McGuigan's left glances off it and sends him to the canvas. The champion has been humiliated. He recovers as best he can, getting up at three and acting as if an unruly banana-skin had just entered his life. McGuigan comes scything his way across the ring, a figure of Death. Pedroza escapes the harvest. He is the coolest man in Loftus Road.

In McGuigan's corner Gerald Hayes is banging the canvas, screaming, 'Feint and throw the right hand.' McGuigan's feint at the end of the seventh was worthy of catching a world champion. He feinted with his head as if he was going to throw a left to the body and then followed up with the big overhand right. Before Pedroza hit the canvas the crowd was on its feet.

The eighth round is Pedroza's best of the fight. He keeps McGuigan at bay with long left jabs and extraordinary counterpunching. Towards the end of the round he exchanges short sharp punches with McGuigan. This man is not going out without a fight.

At the start of the ninth round Pedroza catches McGuigan with a good right. He punches and boxes the same cool round as he did in the eighth, but then lightning strikes again. In almost the identical spot in the ring, McGuigan hits him with another right. McGuigan follows this up with a right to the temple and suddenly Pedroza looks like a Rip Van Winkle who has just woken up with his legs full of pins and needles. He stumbles across the ring. He lurches and tosses, miraculously avoiding the raging torrent that is McGuigan. Somewhere in his head, bells are ringing and blows are falling from all angles. At the end of the round Santiago del Rio is in the ring protesting to Mr Christodoulous that Pedroza has been hit after the bell. He holds up three fingers. Pedroza stands in the centre of the ring and then arches his back like one of the Scots Guards outside Buckingham Palace and heads back to his corner. This proud man is still featherweight champion of the world.

Pedroza slips at the start of the tenth round. He looks at the floor where the dwarf had sprinkled his gold dust as if to say, 'So that's why I've been falling in the same spot.' He has his mind trained so that it is impossible to lose, but his body will not obey. The tenth to thirteenth rounds are purgatorial. In each of them the champion boxes with the fervour of redemption, only to have his potential salvation snatched away at the end.

Pedroza tries his best shots in the thirteenth, hitting McGuigan with a long left and then a strong right hand. McGuigan hits him with another powerful right. By now Pedroza knows the reaction to that particular weapon: grab tight and hold on for dear life. He reaches out and grabs McGuigan with both hands. With pure animal strength McGuigan shrugs him off like a sack of potatoes and hits him with left hooks for his trouble. The referee raises his hands to stop the fight and puts them down as quickly again. Hope is deferred and Pedroza survives the round. At the end of the round Pedroza's corner gives him something that looks like ammonia to revive him.

At the start of the fourteenth Pedroza blesses himself as though it is the last, and then spends most of the round hanging on, determined to go out on his feet. Late in the round Pedroza is crouched low, trying to avoid McGuigan, when suddenly he sees his chance. He shoots a long straight right through McGuigan's guard to the chin. It is the hardest punch he has thrown all night. It is too late.

When Pedroza goes back to his corner at the end of the fourteenth round he sees Eastwood raise three fingers. He is three minutes away from losing his world title. In his corner, McGuigan is asking Eastwood, 'Are you sure I'm ahead?' Eastwood answers, 'You're as far ahead as from here to Belfast.'

Both men touch gloves at the beginning of the fifteenth round. Pedroza behaves with decorum and nobility. He is making his final exit with style. McGuigan ducks and weaves in close to Pedroza. This is what a normal fight looks like in round one.

The three minutes go by on a wave of euphoria. McGuigan is on his way to the world title, but somewhere deep down in him is the fear the verdict might be given against him. Close to the end of the fight he lunges at Pedroza with a Saturday-night special. The distance he misses by is a measure of Pedroza's class as world champion. The bell goes and Pedroza hugs McGuigan. The Eastwood camp are in the ring. Daniel McGuigan watches as Sean McGivern and Ross Mealiff in the company of the whole Eastwood entourage lift McGuigan shoulder high. Pedroza is acknowledging McGuigan as champion, but when his team get into the ring they quickly raise his hand in a last, empty, professional gesture.

Like the Ali–Frazier epics, this fight defies mere professionalism. It's as if the divorce proceedings are over and McGuigan and Pedroza can become friends. There is no doubt that the old champion respects the pretender to his title. The announcement that officially confirms McGuigan as world champion is lost in a huge roar. Possessed young men hurl themselves at the ring as if they could levitate over the hunched journalists. They rise on the substantial backs of the penmen and engulf the ring, searching for McGuigan in an entranced fit.

As McGuigan realizes that the title is officially his, he looks to his brother Dermot as if seeking proof that he won't wake up from this dream. Dermot rubs his head, and for the first time in months I see the fact that Dermot is the elder brother manifest itself.

The TV announcers are trying to get to McGuigan. He thanks everybody, starting off with Mr Eastwood. This man is champion of the world and all the McGuigan charisma starts to come out. He begins to say something about Young Ali: 'One thing I've been thinking about all week. I want to dedicate the fight to the young lad who fought me in 1982.' Suddenly McGuigan starts to falter. It's as if the words 'young lad' have opened up a well that lies too deep for mere words. 'I want to dedicate it to him,' he continues bravely, and then before the eye of the camera he runs ahead of the tears, 'I would not like it to be an ordinary fighter who beat him ...' he says before the tears take centre stage, 'but the world champ.' He has ended in a flood of emotion with the humblest possible affirmation.

Back home in Clones, Irish Television are asking Katie McGuigan if she is proud of her son. 'I'm happy,' she says. 'Pride is not a word I like. Just say I'm happy.'

Amidst the milling crowds McGuigan is led back to his dressing room. Davey Irvine congratulates him. All the rest of the boxers on the bill congratulate him. When he has gone into his own dressing room I ask Davey Irvine how it went. 'Beaten,' he says, 'in the third round.' He pauses. 'Or was it the fourth? That will just tell you how it went. That's it. That's me finished. I'm retired. I'm not tough enough. I hurt too easy.' The amazing thing about Davey Irvine is that there is not an ounce of self-pity or jealousy in his words. He appears as happy as a man can be who has finally resolved some inner truth about himself.

Paddy Byrne comes in and goes straight to Peppy Muir. 'There's your money,' says Paddy. 'I don't know if there's any point in fighting out there, but there's your money anyway. It's bedlam.'

Peppy Muir looks at Paddy and then says, 'I want to fight. I want to be able to say that I fought on the McGuigan bill.' As McGuigan goes upstairs to meet the world's press, Peppy Muir goes out to fight a lonely fight with Simon Eubanks.

I have been with these boxers for two months now and the amazing thing is I have never felt any aggression from any of them. I don't mean aggression towards me, I mean aggression as part of their personality. It's as if they leave all their aggression in the ring. The world of the boxers themselves is a closed silent order where they can communicate with each other with a simple nod of the head.

Upstairs, at the heel of an enormous press throng, one of Gerry Cooney's people keeps asking rhetorically, 'Who trains this guy? I want to meet the man that gets this kid into that condition.'

Brian Eastwood tells him, 'You'll never meet him. We only stop McGuigan getting fit. That's our job – to stop him training too much.'

Cooney's man keeps shaking his head and saying, 'I wish I had fighters like that.'

Ferdie Pacheco, Muhammad Ali's fight doctor, is there. Long ago he recognized the special qualities in McGuigan. He presented McGuigan with his paintings of all the world champions. Ferdie knows talent when he sees it.

McGuigan can never redefine boxing in the way Muhammad Ali did, but he could redefine the definition of sport in this bloody business. He has the talent to be one of the major sportsmen of the second half of the twentieth century. In the midst of all the congratulations McGuigan has one priority: to get Sandra and Blain back to the hotel safely. In the confusion of the night, Sandra forgot to get nappies. The taxi-driver takes her all over London. All the chemists are closed. When he discovers who she is, he insists on taking her home to get a couple of nappies from his own kids.

There is a huge crowd outside the hotel. Eventually McGuigan arrives. He will not join the party. He goes straight up to his room to have a meal. Pat arrives at the celebration, accompanied by Frank Mulligan, Barry's first trainer. Dermot is there, as hoarse as a man suffering from laryngitis. All McGuigan's sisters are there except Rachel, who is keeping her mother company at home.

With all the hype and media attention, somebody some-where was bound to have a nervous breakdown. The part of the McGuigan household in which it happened and the time at which it occurred almost led to a tragedy of Greek dimensions. Phil Coulter had just finished singing 'The town that I love so well', in the Holiday Inn in London when Katie McGuigan and her sister, Bridget Rooney, went to bed in Clones. As Phil sang, Katie switched off the lights one by one. The video-cassette of the fight was still in the machine, stopped where the MC says, 'By a unanimous decision,' and the crowd lets out a deafening roar. At the touch of a tired button, that roar had been stilled. The electrical wiring in the house was making its own silent protest at all the demands being made on it. All night it smouldered with resentment and, as if to time its explosion with the maximum damage, it erupted at five-thirty in the morning after the night before.

What by daytime would have been an inconvenience by night turned into a roaring inferno. Upstairs, Bridget turned over in her sleep. With that sense of alertness that comes from sleeping in strange surroundings, she smelt something amiss. She walked casually down the stairs, to be met by flames in the kitchen. It was too late for do-it-yourself fire-drill. The only thing to do was to try and wake Katie and Rachel, and get them the hell out to safety. By the time Katie had rubbed the sleep from her eyes all of her movable memories had gone up in smoke. Besides what the world knew of Barry, there were all the other little possessions that made her other children as important to her as her most famous son: gone were the pictures of her wedding day; gone were Rebecca's drawings; gone were marriage certificates, birth certificates, everything that proved you existed; and on its way out was the door to Barry's gym, the fire eating its way unconsciously into the heart of a legend. Now the steps were ablaze. Katie backed off.

The fire brigade were on their way. They hadn't far to come but, by the time they arrived, the private part of the McGuigan world was gone. The fire almost split their world in two. The public shop was still there, putting up a brave front as ever. It would be open in a few hours. With a crash the roof caved in on the kitchen. Katie listened to her world collapse. Two dozen handless gloves gave up the fight without any resistance. Muhammad Ali, Alexis Arguello, Jim Watt, all watched their paper worlds ignite and pass away. When the water had washed out what the fire spared, the gym stood lonely and abandoned, perched like a treehouse at the bottom of the yard.

Katie did not want to tell Barry. It would ruin his first day as world champion, but a fire brings hasty news, and Barry found out. Dermot flew home as Barry held the fort at a press conference in the Holiday Inn. He stood out from the rest of the Eastwood camp as he was the only one who could speak without the deep rasp that comes from prolonged abuse of the vocal cords. Hoarse throats were carried round the Holiday Inn like a badge of honour. The English press, with the hyperbole that is an integral part of boxing, told Barry that he had done more than any man to unite Ireland in seven hundred years. No matter which way you calculate it, they were out by a couple of hundred years . . . but then they were only speaking metaphorically. When Barry mentioned that Blain had asked for champ, the pun was lost on the English. The Irish contingent, anxious to hold on to Barry as one of their own, urged him not to explain that 'champ' is a mixture of potatoes and onions. Everybody wanted to claim him.

Barry had meant to stay an extra couple of days, but he decides over dinner to go home to have a look at the damage. In Belfast and Clones, people will try frantically to cope with a schedule whose pace has been set by fire.

At another table Barry Cluskey is telling tales. He is an old family friend. 'I think they even called Barry after me. I was there the day he was born. After the fight people went mad. One fellow was jumping up and down with a towel in his hands. "I got the towel," he says. "I got the towel. Look," says he, and he holds the towel up in my face. "Look," says he, "it's the towel. The blood and all." Don't be showing me that, says I. I've got his fucking nappy.' Cluskey, in the company of about 25,000 others, had a few jars after the fight . . . This had the effect of dislodging his memory somewhat and he ended up in the Grosvenor House Hotel, insisting that he was staying there. He turned round and saw the former champion come through the door. 'I turned round and there was the head and his entourage. I got a surprise, so kind of spontaneously I started to clap and all the people in the lobby started clapping too. Pedroza just froze on the spot and then tears started to come out of his eyes. Down his cheeks. He saw the cross around me neck and he came over and bent down to kiss it. With that his hat fell off. I stood back in surprise like and there was a momentary pause and I didn't know what to do. I got the feeling like that it might be an insult to him to pick it up for him. He bent down to pick it up and he couldn't make it. He couldn't bend down.' Barry's eyes start to mist over. 'What a champ. One of his people came over and picked it up for him. He couldn't bend down with his ribs. That's how much punishment he had taken. Then he put the baseball hat on and just walked away.'

By nine o'clock we are in the VIP lounge at Heathrow. Sandra is doing her best to keep Blain's attention away from the fact that he is exhausted. Behind his dark glasses McGuigan is talking about the fight: 'I couldn't hit him a solid blow. He was slippery. Even the right in the seventh round. It was a good punch but it didn't travel far enough. Then when I swung in the left hook he already had his right hand up so I caught the top of his glove and he fell over with the impact. He said to me that I'd be a great champion. I learned a lot from this fight. I was better than him inside. That's his best aspect, and I was better than him at it. I couldn't throw long lefts with the pain in my elbow. He was hurt. Normally he would grab me inside like a vice.' With two upraised arms Barry imitates the carpenter's tool. 'Then he'd go whap. Grab. See, in the ninth round he didn't grab me, I went whap whap and I could see his legs begin to buckle. Feel that,' McGuigan says. On his chin there is a lump the size of a bull's eye. Barry explains its origin. 'Do you know what round I got that? The fourteenth. I thought I had him going, I could see Christodoulous from the corner of my eye. He made a move as if he was going to stop it and I dropped my guard for a second. Whap. He hit me a straight left.' Barry says it in obvious admiration. 'It was his best shot of the night.' It was the left of a drowning man delivered with all the venom of one fighting for the people of Panama whom he represents. From the silent nodding of heads one gains the impression that the former champion's stock is rising all the time. They begin to realize what Barry has actually accomplished.

On the plane there are two TV crews trying to record Barry's every move. An unsuspecting passenger stops in awed silence for a second before he realizes that his reaction is the centre of attention. Happiness overcomes embarrassment and he rescues himself with one word: 'Barry.' This time it's said not in awe but with a simplicity that means 'I was there'. Saturday, 8 June, is assuming legendary status already. Participation confers a brotherhood on strangers whose nodding silence speaks a religious fervour. What will Belfast be like?

As the plane comes down, people are singing 'Danny Boy', but the melody dies in the expectation of the Belfast welcome. Out on the tarmac nobody is working. Men in overalls stand on top of the Customs Hall waiting for their hero. The press are kept back a respectable distance. Everybody wants a shot of the hero returning home. The walk from the plane to the airport lounge is civilized enough but, once inside the building proper, mayhem becomes the order of the day. People crowd in, trying to touch Barry. There is no point trying to thank his supporters, it's too dangerous. There are certain situations where you must keep going. Danny tries in vain to offer Barry some form of minimal protection. Eventually he arrives at the half-decent sanctuary of a press room. One of the photographers being pushed and jostled moves with a familiar expertise. Hughie Russell is in the front row of men snapping away. It's not quite as dangerous as when he was in the ring with McGuigan, but it's a good workout.

The questions fly at Barry. Yes, he's glad to be home in Belfast. He wants to thank the supporters. He doesn't want to be a flash in the pan. Some question about boxing in general. Barry grabs the opportunity. He thanks all his supporters who have welcomed him home. He points to Russell. 'Especially wee Hughie Russell, my old pal.' Some word in there breaks through the public occasion to the private heart of a man. Hughie turns away. You can't take good photographs with watery eyes. Hughie regains his composure and snaps away.

Outside, Barry's new Lotus waits in the car park. Some question as to whether it's safe to drive it into Belfast. Where is the reception? Outside the offices of the *Belfast Telegraph* and then on to City Hall. Now it's every man for himself.

Outside the *Belfast Telegraph* it's as if the crowd had been reassembled after the fight. The emotion is identical to that at Loftus Road. It's impossible to believe that two nights have passed since McGuigan was crowned world champion. Here it's as if the crowd have been in suspended animation, only to be released from this twilight world by the appearance of their hero. McGuigan jumps on the float and the crowd surge forward with that familiar life of its own. Only this time it's grannies, teenagers, and babes in arms. It seems like all of Belfast has taken the day off. 'Barry, Barry, Barry, Barry,' they keep chanting.

McGuigan is in great form, reaching out to as many as he can touch. One young girl follows the float, hammering all the time at the boards of the makeshift ring. From her deep trance-like depths some demon is being exorcized.

The float has been designed to pass through the gate that blocks the way to that target of targets, City Hall. It only just passes through, forcing those at its sides to a temporary halt. Belfast has been caught unawares but there hasn't been any better improvisation since Van Morrison led a band called Them in the early Sixties. Coloured toilet rolls stand for bunting that defy any political overtones in a city where colour is often a badge of hatred. The political ranting of religious bigots has been shredded from the morning papers into a ticker-tape of snow.

Usually when the T V cameras are on Belfast, the smoke signals in the distance inform an incredulous audience that another car bomb has just exploded in this city of ancient hatred. Today it's different. Today the Romeo and Juliet on the back of the float are not poisoned by family hatred, they are the one speck of hope that the cancer of sectarianism may respond to treatment. When Barry and Sandra hold Blain aloft, the crowd goes wild. At last they have something to cheer about. Still the crowd keeps coming. The ropes and cornerposts of the ring have come asunder, all protection is gone as we gain the sanctuary of City Hall. This is the biggest crowd since Victory in Europe Day, 1945.

Once inside City Hall, Barry insists on speaking to the crowd outside. Barry crawls through a window that has not seen a similar exit since the masons laid the first stone. He picks up the microphone, it fails. No matter, a picture tells a thousand words. Eastwood holds Barry's hand on high and the crowd gives one last united cheer before they journey home to their separate realities.

MONDAY NIGHT

Barry and Sandra get into the Lotus with Blain. They wave goodbye to the City Fathers. A Councillor from the Shankill Road ventures the opinion that Barry could be the first Catholic councillor if he ran against him in the local elections. Barry drives away from that prospect. Eastwood rings his pilot, and within half an hour his son Adrian is driving us to the airstrip at Newtownards. As we sit on the runway ready for take-off, Eastwood whistles a tune, one of those melodies you have heard somewhere before but that you can't quite put your finger on.

We take off and in a couple of minutes we have left the industrialized heartland of Ireland behind. Three minutes' flight time puts paid to the length and breadth of industrialized Ireland. The smokestacks are only a minute behind us when the largest stretch of inland water in Ireland looms up ahead. It's about twenty miles long and ten wide, but our iron bird treats it with disdain. Past Lough Neagh we travel between Cookstown and Donaghmore, respectively Eastwood and McGuigan strongholds.

Somehow the shouting of voices over the roar of the engine brings back memories of Loftus Road. The hoarseness of Brian, Trevor McClintock and Eastwood is in harmony with the mechanical tattoo of the engines. McGuigan's great feat is made greater by a realization of the supporting role played by Pedroza. 'The calibre of the guy he was fighting,' Eastwood suddenly announces, with an emphasis on the word 'calibre' that makes it seem odd in conjunction with a human being. It's as if he wants to compare Pedroza's accuracy with that of a gun and his nerves with its steel. 'Look, I must confess,' he continues, 'after all the trouble the manager put me through, I couldn't help feeling sorry for the fighter. Barry says with the exception of Hagler and Curry, Pedroza is the best pound-for-pound fighter in any division. I say he's better than those two. He's foxier. Only a genius could have stayed up there in the last five rounds. He was kidding to McGuigan the last five rounds. He was gone, but he braved it out.'

The talk centres on the merits of Pedroza for a minute, but Eastwood wants to take the conversation higher. 'There is something different about this, about the whole McGuigan phenomenon. I've seen some great sporting occasions. I won an All-Ireland medal myself, but this is different. The emotion of it, it's an emotional thing. I don't cry, I never cry, but I saw people today at the City Hall and they couldn't stop crying. Girls, ladies, all crying. It wasn't just the women. I saw three or four lads from the Shankill. I know two of them, just got out of Long Kesh, and they were crying. Big baby tears rolling down their face. It's bigger than any of us. It must be this peace thing. Barry's supporters are not boxing people. It's the people who live up in Lesson Street want a bit of peace.'

Eastwood is whistling the same melody again. I know I have heard it somewhere before but I just can't remember where. Somewhere to our right as we begin our descent is

Boa Island. On it is a carved statue which pre-dates Christian Ireland. One of its heads looks north and the other looks south. It's stuck there on an island in the middle of Lough Erne for no particular reason. A two-headed idol with eyes in the back of both his heads.

As we drive into Clones the roads for miles around are lined with parked cars. People are coming from all over. It's like a scene from the Bible, thousands of people converging on this tiny little Irish town. The town itself is a mass of bunting and flags. Each trade and shop has contributed its own sign. The butcher's shop in Fermanagh Street has 'We steak the lot on you Barry' emblazoned across its front. Up the street the Italian fish and chip shop has 'It's a pizza cake', one of the drapers has 'Sock it to him Barry'.

The Diamond has never seen such a crowd in its history. The whole square is full. From an open-ended truck, officials are addressing the crowd. When Barry comes on stage he starts to thank everybody, even the Monaghan team who won the league a couple of months before and whom he hadn't had a chance to congratulate. It's almost become a joke, this congratulating of Barry's. Somebody told him he might be going overboard once. He listened for a long time and then said, 'If you're telling me to stop congratulating the people I want to, then I will just start by saying somebody told me I sound foolish congratulating everybody and maybe I do but still these are the people I want to congratulate.' McGuigan does not really mind if his genuine emotions upset people. The way he sees it, they have the problem and not him. For a time the crowd seems to be getting out of control, the people coming in from the outlying countryside continually pushing those at the front nearer the stage. McGuigan makes an appeal for everybody to take two steps back and they do, almost in unison: about thirty or forty rows of people step back calmly and in order.

After the orations we slip into the local library, which will lead us by another entrance to the back of the McGuigan shop. We go into the yard to see the fire damage.

It's much worse than we expected. Where the kitchen used to be is a black heap of ashes. It's as if some cruel fate in the midst of triumph has raped and pillaged his past.

Sandra starts to cry. Pat McGuigan is leading us through the debris as if our visitation could somehow bring back the past. 'Everything I worked for,' he says simply.

At twelve forty-five we are again on the runway in Enniskillen. In absolute darkness we take off. There is a sadness about this leg of the journey; leaving McGuigan is like leaving the Land of Youth. For a couple of weeks leading up to the fight and for a time after it, nothing mattered. Time stood still . . . a land of eternal youth where we could all play out our childhood fantasies through this extraordinary young man called McGuigan, the last of the cool clean heroes. A boyhood hero stepped from the comics of our childhood, fearless, strong and full of insane life. No comic-strip writer would have the audacity to pen McGuigan's story as it happened. Even they have respect for the boundaries of soap opera. The man who is sitting beside me is bursting at the seams with fulfilment. The tune he is whistling is the Panamanian national anthem. For ever and a day they will remember McGuigan. Whenever boxing is spoken of, somebody will eventually say, 'But do you remember Barry McGuigan?' Everybody will. Some old wag in the corner will lean forward and say, 'Who was the man behind him? What was his manager's name?' He will pause with all the confidence of one who knows and say: 'McGuigan and Eastwood, sure there was never another team like them.'

Eastwood says little on the flight. He's thinking of the future. 'How many of us depend on McGuigan? Look at the team of us. There must be thirty people close to him – and when he goes, we go. There's no need for Ned doing the ring, no need for Harry O'Neill, no need for wee Billy Barnes, no need for a sponsor, no need for a manager. When he loses his title everybody's shagged, and we're back to porridge again.'

Suddenly, in the immense blackness we are flying

through, an oasis of light appears below us. 'What's that?' I inquire.

The pilot, Tom Tuke, looks out. 'Oh, that's Long Kesh,' he says.

Until there are one million Barry McGuigans Ulster will never sleep.